First published by Serpent's Tail in 2004.

Published by Semiotext(e)
PO BOX 629, South Pasadena, CA 91031
www.semiotexte.com

Cover photo: Cady Noland, *The Mirror Device* (detail), 1987. Photo by Fabian Frinzel. © Cady Noland

Design: Hedi El Kholti

10 9 8 7 6 5 4 3 2 1

ISBN: 978-1-63590-204-4

Distributed by The MIT Press, Cambridge, Mass. and London, England
Printed in the United States of America

Notice

Heather Lewis

Introduction by Melissa Febos

semiotext(e)

Heather Lewis was not the role model my parents would have chosen for me, but she was my ideal. Queer, determined, brilliant, and *tall*, I would definitely have thrown myself at her had we ever met. We overlapped in New York during the last years of her life, which were my first in the city, but I was still a teenager and we surely bought our drugs from different vendors, brought them home to different scenes. If I'd arrived a few years earlier and gotten sober quicker, we might have sat in the same church basements in the Village.

The year I was born, she was a freshman at Sarah Lawrence College, twenty-four years before I'd get there. Her mentor, Allan Gurganus, describes seeing her in riding boots during a cocktail hour for students, parents, and faculty. He took her for a boy, at first. She was like the women I located all my life as best friends, lovers, and heroes. The sort I wanted to be, whose "eyes seemed wise, at some cost."

I was ambitious like her and, even before I read her, aspired to write similar work. I wanted to name things I had not been given words for, to articulate the unspeakable in hope of inuring myself to it. I liked reading hard books and I liked to write things I could never have said out loud. I still do. My young efforts were often shocking, sexual, and grotesque. I wanted to annihilate my own innocence, before I realized how precious it was. That, Lewis and I didn't share.

When I read her debut novel, *House Rules*, I loved the tough and lucid voice of its fifteen-year-old narrator, Lee, who confessed, "I'd like it better if you thought I just know how things work so work them." Like Lee and Lewis, I had passed for eighteen when I was fifteen, and got up to trouble with people much older. I also liked you to think I *worked* things, rather than was worked by "this stuff [that] follows me around and once it starts I can't move till it's over."

House Rules is a hypnotic and brutal novel—drawn from Lewis's experience as an incest survivor, addict, and competitive show jumper—in which the young riders are treated similarly to the livestock: as assets that can be better controlled with chemical substances. The sex in *House Rules* is copious, violent, and arousing. It scared me, and I couldn't look away.

In that regard, Lewis's first book has nothing on *Notice*. In it, a young sex worker who trolls a suburban train station for tricks becomes embroiled with a sadistic man and his alternately complicit and nurturing wife. The three reenact the death of the couple's daughter, who was molested and murdered by her father. The unnamed narrator of *Notice* is essentially Lee a few years older, and like in *House Rules*, her story is full of violent sex, assault, and plenty in the murky realm between. It is also preoccupied with the dynamic of a destructive triad, the love of a woman who fails to protect her. When she tries to escape the couple, the man has her institutionalized and a sordid trajectory unspools.

In Gurganus's assessment, the book's "truest subject is the cost of early sexual violation," and it's hard to disagree. Lewis's father, her abuser, haunts all of her writing. He is, in the words of Lewis's longtime partner Ann Rower: "The grand villain of the piece—of all the pieces she ever wrote, every interview she ever gave, every thought she had, every breath she took." Rereading the book was alternately arousing and sickening. Middle age finds me more penetrable than I was as a younger reader and I often had to put the novel down. It has one of the hardest endings of any book I've read. I also felt more alive in its pages than I have reading anything in a long time.

Lewis began seeking a publisher for *Notice* in 1996, but the content was too much for the eighteen editors she queried—"too close to their notions of the author's actual experience," Dale Peck suggested in his 2005 review of the book for *New York* Magazine. The events are so brutal and relentless that, as Gurganus writes, "we wish to believe it is happening solely on the level of Allegory." Any knowledge of the author's life makes such wishes impossible. Rower writes that even many of Lewis's close friends couldn't stomach the book. It wasn't just the sexual violence that readers struggled with, but the flattened tone. "Heather's genius creation," writes Rower, "was the voice of a horribly abused young woman who spoke dispassionately about the shocking scenes of her own abuse." Only fellow survivors could appreciate it. Lewis was devastated by the book's rejection and never saw it published. Thanks to editor Amy Scholder, it was finally released posthumously in 2004, by Serpent's Tail, ten years after Lewis had written it.

Her second published volume ended up being her third written. Acquired by Nan Talese and published by Doubleday in 1998, *The Second Suspect* was the third installment in what Lewis considered a trilogy. She transplanted much of *Notice*'s plot (and one notable scene) into the novel, "filtering the central conceit of incest, misogyny, and murder through a detective's objective gaze," as Dale Peck wrote, "rather than the unnerving subjectivity of a survivor."

As in *Notice*, a rich suburban man with a complicit wife (who shares the name of the wife in *Notice*) has murdered a sex worker after using her to reenact the molestation and murder of their daughter. The real heroine of the book is recognizable as a slightly more aged version of the narrator(s) of Lewis's previous two books. "Carver" carries the memories and scars of *Notice*'s brutalities, and it is her testimony that finally pins the culprit.

The Second Suspect was supposed to be a blockbuster but it was panned by critics, who interpreted its shocking violences as immature and insinuated that serious art could not comprise such transgressive and disturbing elements. How devastating it must have felt to have her work so misunderstood, yet again. In the wake of this disappointment, Lewis relapsed after many years of sobriety, suffered a mental breakdown, and committed suicide in 2002, at the age of forty.

In 1999, Joan Larkin edited an anthology of queer women writers' coming-out stories, *A Woman Like That*. It is long out of print, but I found a battered copy in a used-book outlet. It includes an essay by Lewis that to classify as a "coming-out story" is almost laughable. It describes the long and excoriating series of events that made up her childhood, which included middle school addictions; affairs with adult women that began during adolescence; her father's committing her to psychiatric institutions to "cure" her, a hobby "he worked at with vindictive precision" after they ended up interested in the same woman; and her sexual relationship with a therapist she calls "Beth," and later another older woman named "Ingrid," details that were lifted almost wholesale from her life and used in *Notice*, replete with these names.

Near the end of the essay, she describes a male doctor to whom her father sent her for years. This doctor diagnosed her as "a Virginia Woolf type time bomb. I'd certainly kill myself by forty." Which, of course, she did. Nearly everything in the essay can be found in her books. It seemed like such a Rosetta stone to her work, and to *Notice* in particular, that my hands trembled after I'd finished reading it. I had suspected that her fiction was pretty true to life. As Rower writes, "I know most of what I know about Heather from her writing." Still, the confirmation shook me. I had still held out some hope for allegory.

The transparent use of autobiography in fiction—so-called *confessional* work—has long been denigrated by many critics and readers, as if any suggestion of catharsis precludes the aesthetic value of such art. Now, we have the "autofiction" loophole, for memoirists who want to be taken seriously. The power of combing through one's trauma and transforming it into art, of course, is a proven method of psychological integration. Whether the art will be any good or not is a separate question. Lewis's is good. Her transparent use of events and dynamics from her own life is as thrilling to read now, decades later, as it is unsettling. "As with the New Narrative writers who preceded her," writes Peck, "Heather saw no difference between experience and our representations of it." She could have tried something else (to some extent she did, in *The Second Suspect*), but the work she was committed to doing on the page, that insisted she make it, was irrefutable. She was incapable of pandering, of defanging her instincts.

In a 1996 interview with bell hooks, the artist Camille Billops argued that one of the most revolutionary things an artist can do is make work about their own life. "Put all your friends in it, everybody you loved, so one day they will find you and know that you were all here together," she said. Lewis unabashedly did that and she included not only her friends but her abusers, her lovers, her doctors, and some who were all three. When we aren't calling them "narcissistic," we like to call the artists who do this "brave," but I know it has less to do with bravery than necessity, and nothing to do with narcissism. The brave part is mostly done by readers who meet the work on the page, face its hard truth, and recognize its value.

I've been thinking a lot about lineage lately. Lewis is unequivocally part of my artistic lineage, and many others, including one of queer writers who straddle the line of horror and the erotic, who are kin across genres. I'm thinking of Dennis Cooper, A. M. Homes, Samuel R. Delany, and so many others. I don't see this kind of work much anymore outside of the horror or thriller genres and wonder if we have lost something in our squeamishness, our fear of irreducible complexity and of bad faith readers.

What we do see today is a fleet of young, jaded narrators with detached voices. But there is a neutered quality to today's young, fucked-up narrators, no matter how avid their sex lives. So often, theirs is an affect, a style, steeped in irony, and sure, I believe it makes the pains of such characters' lives easier, but it has not the stakes of a Lewis narrator. They aren't cool and detached because the only alternative is to go up in flames.

It was a familiar experience in my youth, to read a book and feel ravaged by it, just completely fucked up and flabbergasted. To encounter a book in which eroticism and violence and trauma and pathos mingled dangerously. These books didn't explain themselves, or apologize, or offer a tidy reward of hope at the end, a narrative that reduced their frightful ambiguities to some comforting pathology.

I'm not sure I could handle reading such books today, but I wish there were still room for them to exist.

Fuck that doctor. It was not Lewis but her art that was a time bomb. This book, in particular. It is set to detonate in the minds of readers, generation after generation. To remind us how hard and pure a truthful work of art can be. Here. Brace yourself.

Notice

One

For the longest time I didn't call it turning tricks. When I'd leave work, cross the street to the train station and, if some guy—man, I guess really you'd call him—had come off the train, was on his way home, I'd take his money.

We'd do it in his car. I'd work maybe twenty minutes. Get maybe twenty dollars, which was good compared to what I made at my job across the street. Besides, it's hard to get more in a car. At least I told myself this. Though I guess how much depends on what you'll do for it.

I wouldn't do a whole lot; acted pretty grumpy about doing anything. But then they liked that, one or two of them especially did.

This wasn't something I was looking to do, though by how easy it happened you would've said it was. People have. Still, for me it happened by accident. And while it's true I needed the money that's not all I needed from it. I don't care what anybody says. I understand the reason for telling people that, people outside it. But the thing is, I could never really see anyone as outside it. What the extra need is, the thing besides money? I've never pinned it down. I know it's there, though.

So anyway, every day after work I'd wait. Well, maybe not every day, not at first. Gradually it got to be that regular. And then I got regulars. By then it becomes a two-way thing with them depending on you and you depending on them. Once it's there, who's to blame doesn't matter because you're each getting what you came for.

Maybe it started because I didn't want to go home. Home right then meant my parents' house. It hadn't meant that in a long time and to have it mean that again, so late in the game, relatively, wasn't easy or even simple.

I had, after all, picked the Juvey place over them, but that had turned out nasty. Worse than I'd thought and I'd thought bad. Of course, I'd had a shaky start there and after that was marked. This didn't feel new to me, but the way they went about reminding you daily and in such obvious ways, the way they made you a dog, put a leash on you—and I mean this literally—I had to get out no matter where I'd end up.

I'd ended up at home with a capital H, and so every day after work I avoided going there. This despite the fact my parents weren't living there and wouldn't be for months. It didn't matter. Everything in the place belonged to them. Nothing much belonged to me. They'd tossed my stuff when I got locked up. Anyway, as long as I stayed there it seemed I belonged to them too and I needed not to be reminded of this.

For quite a while I'd gone to a bar after work. One across the street, catercorner to the station. Soon enough that turned into a thing with one of the bartenders. This was based not even on sex but on cocaine and, that not being my favorite drug, I tired of it fast.

Maybe somehow I figured if I hung around outside the bar instead of inside I'd get paid instead of paying, or trading. Trading, anyone will tell you, ranks as low as you can go and already I'd had years of it. Been born to it really. And so I felt the need to move up. Or I needed to make things plainer.

So I did move up, which meant out, or never going in—the bar, that is. I don't know when the first time was, though I do remember it. And like always, like everyone else, I was thinking, Well, maybe just this once.

The reason it's never just once is the same reason money's only a part of it. Most anyone can take or leave that, though they don't think they can. The cover story of all time, that's what money is. The excuse of excuses no one will question because they so much need to use it themselves.

The first one, I didn't want him to know he was first. Even before it was actual work I didn't want anyone to think they were first.

Later, of course, it becomes good business to convince them all it's your first time, first time for money anyway. Not too many would believe beyond that. And when even that becomes impossible to sell, then you try to convince them they're different, or that what they're asking for is.

Always you try and convince them you like it, or them, whichever seems more important. Unless they could care less about that stuff. Those are the easiest in a way, well, depending.

But that actual first time it's not so likely you'd want him knowing, unless there's someone else in it to profit. And I'd promised myself I'd never have someone like that.

So that first time happened by standing around. By walking past the bar instead of going in. And then past my car and not driving home. It was awkward, but more for the guy off the train. Wasn't his first time, that I could tell, but probably his first time this close to home.

Once I saw his hands, the way they fiddled with his wallet, I didn't so much relax as switch. We were still talking about him buying me a drink. He was asking how much that would cost and worrying about the cash he had on him.

I don't know, maybe he thought we were talking about a motel. I wasn't. Knew while I'd cost more, I'd pay more, so I wasn't going any farther than this parking lot. I just wanted him to show me his car.

Finally he said, "Where do we go?"

So I said, "You got a car?" And that was that. That part was settled.

The car was nice, nice for this. One of those ones with a front seat that moves back all in one piece. Not so good for driving, but good for sitting in.

Like I said, he didn't know how to act, so he started walking me around to the passenger side. He stopped somewhere near the hood ornament.

Anyway, he let me walk the rest of the way by myself and I got to my door before he got to his. Had to wait for him to pop the locks.

I was wearing kind of a short skirt. He had on a suit, a light-weight one sort of olive-colored. It was almost too late for dressing this way, too far into fall. Far enough that I was wearing stockings, black ones, the kind with a seam up the back.

I guess what I'm saying is we both looked the part and that made things easier. Easier for me at least. And he was young and not bad looking, and this helped me too.

I'd gotten my money already, outside the car. Not much left to do now but do him, so I put my hand in his lap. Got him the rest of the way there, then unzipped him. Touched him some before I put my head down.

It was fine really, was no big deal. He took maybe four minutes, and when he came I swallowed because neither of us had planned any place else to put it. Besides he'd been decent so it seemed wrong to leave him a mess to clean up.

I didn't wait around, mostly because I could tell he didn't want me to. I just got out of his car and started walking to mine, then kept walking past it again.

Wound up going into the bar after all.

I spent some of the twenty drinking because the bartender I knew came in late. Once he got there I stayed as long as he did. Sat at the bar until they closed. Then sat at a table until he finished locking up, counting the drawer, drying some glasses.

When he got done, he came over. He pushed aside the table I sat behind. Got down on his knees so he was in between mine. Afterward we did maybe half a gram, though it was more like speed cut with coke than vice versa and this wasn't the first time. Still, I wasn't ready to start anything over it. Not yet. Just noticed and knew I'd have to say something sometime soon.

My end of this deal had been short to begin with and was now getting shorter. Like I said, I'd seen I was paying too much for too little. I guess getting paid out there in the parking lot made me really feel it. Before it'd been more of an idea.

I guess you'd call this a transitional period.

Two

The transition didn't last very long. Lasted only until this new one walked up to me. It couldn't have been more than a few weeks later.

I went with him a few times there in his car before he asked me to come home with him. That's not something I'd usually agree to, never had in fact. I'd made up my mind not to when I began this. But he was kind of a rough guy, which made it harder to refuse. Not for the reasons you might think, but because that thing pulls me. And then, too, he'd dangled a carrot, which was his wife.

So we drove to his place. It couldn't have been even ten miles from the station. Going up the driveway seemed to take longer than getting there.

Once inside he sat me down on the living room couch with a drink and then called his wife to join us. I couldn't tell yet how he wanted it played so I stayed put—drank my drink, smoked my cigarette, and kept quiet.

His wife was good looking, nothing suburban or matronly going on, which was a decided relief. I looked her over pretty carefully because I knew he'd want at least that much. She acted shy of me, fidgety. He'd told her to expect me, or to expect something. I could tell by what she was wearing—a long black negligee that trailed a little behind her when she crossed the room.

She sat down beside me. I still waited for my cue, didn't touch her. I understood they'd scripted things this far and so I put out my cigarette, not wanting it to get in the way.

The wife touched my cheek, still awkward and shaky like she was trying to find the right way to go about it. When her fingers got to my neck I found myself borrowing her shivers. Found myself trembling all over and so already I knew this was not a good thing to pursue. That it would make me feel something, which naturally is about the last thing you want.

I turned my head away so I didn't have to look anywhere near her eyes, great big brown eyes I could tell were sad every night and not just this one, not just because of this. Hers was the last sort of headset I needed to slip into. I knew I couldn't afford to get that kind of sloppy around her husband.

By now she'd begun touching my breasts so I took off my shirt, left my bra on because he told me to. He told me to hike up my skirt and open my legs, and I did these things too. All this time I looked at my bag. I'd put my underwear in there when he'd had me take it off in the car. I'd put the first half of the money there too.

Not looking at his wife didn't exactly solve all my problems. She'd solved some of hers though, and was no longer so hesitant. She'd slid onto my lap, was facing me. By then I had to turn my head back to her and besides, like I said, not looking wasn't working anyway.

I took the negligee off her shoulders, began to kiss her there, held her around the waist and she let the negligee drop.

Her husband, by now he'd sat down. I could catch sight of him over her shoulder. Could smell his cigarette, hear the ice in his glass.

At first, closing my eyes helped. But I found I liked keeping them open better. Felt safer that way.

She was wearing one of those female-lingerie things I couldn't name. All I know is you unbuttoned the front of it. Well, I did. She started to take off my bra, but her husband still didn't want this. And he didn't want us lying down on the couch either. What he wanted was her on the floor on her knees and everything taken off her.

This was the point I got nervous, began searching for a way out. But I had no idea why because what she did to me now had me leaning back one minute and grasping her the next—back and forth like this until he got out of his chair.

The only thing he took off was his belt. He put it around her waist and pulled up. This made her stop what she was doing to me and that made him mad, or gave him the excuse. He'd gotten down behind her and was pulling harder on the belt, was rubbing against her, pressing into her. She'd laid her head across my lap and I was holding on to her. I put my fingers into her mouth because I didn't like how she sounded. I couldn't listen to it.

When he put his dick in her ass she grabbed hold of me. She had her arms around my waist, her head tucked into my stomach. I probably should have held her too, but instead I tried pulling away, but getting leverage was impossible. It was then I noticed him watching me.

He fucked her methodically. Slammed her pretty good, and it was clear this hurt her. She was crying into my skirt. But the look on his face? There was nothing there, a hint of a smile but that was it. Maybe that's why I was trying to get away.

He hadn't paid me enough to watch something like this. He'd paid me enough to do it to me, but not to watch him do it to her.

And if this sounds like a pure thought, understand it as purely self-serving. Believe me, getting it would've been way the hell easier.

When he'd finished with her, we left her there on the floor. I put my shirt back on, picked up my bag, followed him out to his car. I knew we weren't done yet because he hadn't come off. Turned out, he was always like this—he got his money's worth always.

Now, outside, he took my bag from my hand. Put it on the hood of the car and then pressed my head down beside it. He held my hands together behind my back and I didn't mind any of this. I was kind of sleepy about it and didn't struggle. I just waited.

I felt his dick through his pants before he took it out and then I felt it between my legs, rubbing me. He let go of my hands. I tried to find something to hold on the hood of his car, but couldn't. There was nothing there. And so when he pulled me back, I turned my face into my bag because it smelled smokey and leathery; it smelled familiar.

I don't know whether this would've happened without having his wife, but when he fingered me I got edgy. I knew he was bringing me close and I didn't think I could stop it. Worse, I knew he could tell. Not that he said anything. He didn't have to. What he did was put his dick in my cunt and not my ass. And this not being his style made it clear to me he really wanted to be sure.

I didn't take long once he'd done that. And though I was silent about it, I knew he felt it by the little tug he gave my hair. And just to ice it, he pulled out. Jerked himself. Had his dick up close to my ass when he did this, but then slipped it away. Pulled my skirt down and leaned into me.

This wasn't entirely new. He always jerked himself. But he'd hand me his handkerchief, let me clean myself off. Tonight, though, he was rubbing me in it. Tonight, he wanted me taking this home.

After, he walked around and got in the car. I wasn't completely sure I could move but I did. Moved my hand first, toward my bag, and then moved the rest of me. And while my legs were shaky, there wasn't too far to go.

I opened the door and sank into the seat. He started the car. I had my bag on my lap and was rummaging for a cigarette. Soon as I'd lit it, he took it from me and so I had to start over. We didn't say anything, not until we got out on the road. Then he was asking where to drop me because before we'd always been in that parking lot.

That's where I should've gone back to. My car was still there and I knew it wasn't good for him to know where I lived. My faculties let me down, though. And there he was suggesting he just drop me at home. "Wherever that is," he said.

So this man, this regular, he drives me right up to my door. And without me having to ask he gives me the rest of my money. And though I'm thinking it's not enough and never again, instead we're making another date, and he's saying he'll pick me up here instead of the train station, and while this is all bad precedent I'm agreeing.

Three

Walking into my parents' house felt even worse than it should have so I headed straight for the living room, for the bar in there. Open their liquor cabinet and the smell of gin is enough to knock you to your knees. I'm used to it, though. I got out a bottle of vodka, opened it and poured a short one into the nearest glass. My parents are not the highball type, tall glasses I guess being frivolous.

Now I had the drink, I put my bag down on the coffee table and dropped onto the couch. I was thinking how at their house—the couple—there was no coffee table, nothing in front of the couch to block his view.

The date I'd arranged was two days off, which occurred to me meant the weekend. Well, Friday night. I still had my day job, the one I was supposed to go to in the morning, but this seemed less and less likely.

I began taking things out of my bag. First the cigarettes, then my lighter, then the cash. Laid the four new and now-wrinkled hundreds across the table. I nicked the edge of one with my cigarette, and I might have kept it burning, except I'm a little too practical for that. Last I took out my underwear.

If he wanted a weekend, we'd have to talk about money. But the problem was he'd pay it. This was why he'd become such a staple. The reason I told myself anyway. The excuse for why I did and let him do things I'd never agreed to with the others. I mean, the very first time he'd gotten me in the backseat on my stomach and for just forty bucks. Then I wised up and told him that sort of thing cost more.

I poured another drink and took it to bed, that and the cigarettes. The rest I left spread across the table. I didn't sleep a great deal, and when it got light I thought it'd be easy to just get up and go to work. I'd planned to wear the same skirt. That was the hitch, the thing reminding me that maybe something had actually happened or changed.

I'd been keeping my regular job for all the reasons you always hear. The convenient division between night and day. A way to insist nothing's unusual.

I was nearly out of the house before I remembered my car wouldn't be there. I got as far as dialing a taxi and then as far as the train station, but what I did then was get into my car and drive home.

I called in sick that day. It was the next day I told them I quit. Asked them to mail me my check. I spent both of these days half-asleep. Was really just waiting for his car in the driveway, and before I heard it I put some extra clothes in my bag in case things dragged out.

We didn't talk about money and he didn't give me any up front. Just on principle this was something I should've challenged but didn't.

Once we'd gotten to his house, the two of us sat downstairs for a bit, though this time you could tell we'd be going upstairs. I'm not exactly sure why we were killing this stretch of time but since I wasn't in a questioning mood, I let this pass too.

When we did go up the stairs he stopped at the landing, began pointing out pictures of his children. One daughter in particular he said I reminded him of, and I thought, At least for now you're doing to me what you want to be doing to her. At least she's off at some school like the rest of them.

We continued up the stairs and into their bedroom. His wife was taking a bath. She'd left the bathroom door open, so from the tub she could see us come in.

He told me to sit on the bed, on the edge so I faced her. He sat in a chair opposite, a straight-backed one that looked like it didn't belong in here. This chair was against the wall, near the doorjamb and so his wife could see me. And she could see that he could see me, but she couldn't really see him, not more than his elbow.

I sat there waiting because I knew he liked giving instructions. I hadn't worn any underwear this time because, let's just say, I learn fast. He'd reached over to me in the car, smiling when he'd discovered this. It was the sort of thing I thought might get me more cash. It might with someone like him who liked you paying attention.

So anyway, when he told me to touch myself I didn't have to take anything off. And I didn't even consider unbuttoning my shirt or anything like that because already I knew that was part of it to him. Having me dressed and her not.

It seemed odd that I could see both of them. It should've given me some kind of command but instead I felt nervous. I looked first at him. But then my eyes went to her. When that happened, he said, "You look at me."

He'd carried his drink up here. Was still holding it and so that's what I focused on. But he didn't like that either. He said, "At me," again and louder so I knew to meet his eyes.

I was beginning to think his eyes never changed. That they looked this same way always—guarded but not entirely cold, not quite closed off. There's so much more someone like this can accomplish if he keeps himself just that little bit open.

That's the pull. And the kicker, too. That it's absolutely you he's fucking with. Not anyone else. That's the thing you've probably always wanted. Someone's undivided attention. And you've wanted it so much and for so long that the form it takes no longer matters.

So he was holding my eyes and I was holding myself. But I wasn't doing much of anything. I knew that couldn't last long. Still, I needed to get my bearings because he wasn't going to just let me pretend it all and be done.

"Come on, now," he said, and so already I'd used too much time.

Out of the corner of my eye I tried to find his wife. From the little I could see she hadn't moved a muscle since we came in. And while I knew how she'd gotten that way—I understood it completely—I still couldn't figure what would cow a person so. I mean look, will you, at who's saying this.

Without him telling me to, I leaned back some, opened my legs more. I started touching myself in a way that seemed to help all of us.

He stayed in his chair for the longest time and so I was caught in limbo, not sure how far to take myself. But then finally he got up. Did that same thing of taking off his belt, only this time he put it around my neck. This didn't feel so bad as you might think. Not at first it didn't.

He stayed standing in front of me. I was looking where his belt used to be until he tugged on it. Until he pressed himself into my face but with his pants still zipped, which left me licking cloth.

He pulled at me with the belt some and pulled my hair a little too. I couldn't see anything but knew what his wife saw. I found myself wondering how things between them had gotten here. Or if they'd always lived this way, and I was just one of many they'd tried.

Thinking this way made me a little too nervous and so I started to unzip his pants. Did this to have something more to do, but he stopped me. Put my hands back between my legs where they hadn't been in a while.

He unzipped his pants. I kept touching myself even though I knew he'd put my hands there simply to keep them away from him. That was the real trouble—him playing my end better than me.

He put his dick in my mouth and still the only thing he let me touch was myself. That made him the one keeping me upright—doing this by yanking his belt and my hair. It wasn't the most comfortable arrangement anymore but each time I went to put my arms behind me, just to help prop myself up, he smacked me. So I'm getting it slow, but I'm getting it.

He had his legs between mine, nudging them apart, and was hard enough now to take up most of my throat. Between that and the belt, breathing wasn't so easy.

When he took his dick back, I got a pretty good breath but I couldn't get it past the belt. He pushed me down. Had his hand on my chest now, and so there wasn't any place for the air to go anyway.

I'd left my hands where he'd put them and his were there, too, opening me up, sliding his dick in. Soon as he'd done that, he took hold of my wrists, held them down at my sides. His dick helped me by the way it hurt. Kept me from thinking anything for a while until it got where it didn't hurt, but did the opposite. When that happened I couldn't stay with him anymore.

Like he knew this, he pushed my arms over my head. Caught hold of his belt again too, so that each time he hit into me, he choked me. This wasn't the way he usually fucked me, though I expect it's the way he usually fucked her. The other night he was showing her what he'd been doing to me, and now was showing me what she got.

I wasn't used to having his face near mine and here he was staring right into my eyes with that same look as when I'd watched him do her. I couldn't hold his gaze. Closed my eyes and opened my mouth; figured having his tongue there would be okay, that it was something I needed, that I needed something to suck on. But none of this mattered because he wasn't thinking it, I was.

He said, "Don't you look away from me. Don't you ever."

I opened my eyes and it meant I felt all of it. Felt his dick up in me and worse than before because now he held it nearly still. Moved just a little until I found my eyes closing again, my legs wrapping around him. Until I found myself pressing against him.

"Look at me," he said, but this time not harsh. This time nearly teasing, putting me in a place in myself I thought would break me apart. And again like he knew, he let off me and got up. Left his belt around my neck but let go of it. Left me to turn on my side and pull my legs up underneath me, left me clutching myself.

He got his wife out of her bath. Brought her in still wet and laid her down on her stomach right next to me. Then he lifted her up on her knees and after that I stopped watching. And I pretended I didn't feel anything either. I even got up, took his belt off and went and sat in his chair, finished his drink, lit a cigarette, and wondered how long he'd let me do these sorts of things.

Sitting there behind them I still wasn't watching. Out the window you could see their pool lit up in the dark. That's what I stared at. This didn't keep me from hearing her, though. I'd found no way to stop that, but if I looked hard enough at the water it muffled her some.

It was me he jerked off on—my face and my neck, while I still sat in his chair. He'd caught me off guard, what with the way I'd put myself out on the lawn and so already I knew that solution had limits.

Soon as he came, he went into the bathroom, which meant I couldn't go in there, couldn't clean him off me without searching the house. And what with the state I was in, with what I'd been trying to maintain, that was just too far to go.

His wife had the bedspread pulled up around her and seeing her this way I realized we hadn't been alone before. That we'd never been introduced. And then I asked her her name and she said, "Ingrid." All of this happened before I'd had a chance to think whether her name would be a good thing to know. Already I knew it wasn't. As soon as she said it, I knew. And I liked her voice, which could only make everything more difficult.

She watched the bathroom door pretty intently, never let her eyes leave it for long. I stayed planted in that chair, though I took my shirt off, used it to clean myself. I kept trying to pretend I didn't want to go and lie down with her. I understood this was why he was taking so long to come back. That he wanted to see us together when he walked in again.

I looked at the pool some more. Lit another cigarette and just about when I thought I wasn't going to, I got up and went to her, sat beside her and let her smoke through my fingers. Other than that I didn't touch her.

She touched me, though. She seemed to want to undress me because she kept running her hand under my bra the way someone does before they unfasten it. So far, I hadn't even taken off my shoes, nothing but my shirt and I'd had a reason for that.

I stopped her hand, got up to put out the cigarette, though I didn't have to. There was another ashtray right there on the nightstand. She asked me my name and I gave her the one I use in these situations. I felt a strange twinge, though, as if somehow I owed her the truth.

She said, "So, Nina, did you come here only for him?" And when I didn't answer she said, "I asked him to bring you. He brought you for me."

I think she said "brought." She might have said "bought," I'm not sure. The thing I do know for sure is women do everything differently, though not so much so you can't catch it.

I took off my skirt but just stood there, still in my shoes and stockings, and the bra I hadn't let her take off me. I was trying to decide how hard a time to give her. But this wasn't something I ever did with the men. When I realized this I slipped off the shoes and lay down with her.

I wasn't sure how she wanted it. The men always say. Not real clearly, but enough so you know what they mean. She didn't say anything. She tucked me under the bedspread and helped me out of my bra.

I lay back because she wasn't letting me do anything, not right off. I let myself close my eyes again. This was something I wanted to do all of the time with all of the men, but I never chanced it. And here I was tonight giving in to it over and over. Giving in, though it should've been clear these two put me more at risk than anyone I'd ever encountered.

And it should've been clear by now, too, which of them put me most at risk. Still, I couldn't help it. Her mouth on me had me needing too much to care and so even when I heard the door, knew he'd come in, I kept my eyes closed.

Her concession was to push the bedspread off us. And I was glad for it because it'd gotten too warm under there. She kept up her lead, which still wasn't how I thought it should play. She kept me off balance, kept me flat on my back.

She'd taken off my stockings and so I had nothing on. He didn't have to say a word for her to begin nudging me over. She did this a little at a time, until we lay across the bed instead of lengthwise.

I knew what his view was, and then she moved so she lay by my side instead of on top of me. I didn't exactly care but it wasn't so far from my mind anymore—him watching us. Maybe it never had been. I can't say it really bothered me. I just thought it should.

She still kissed my breasts, was moving her hand across the top of my thighs, anywhere but in between them until I couldn't keep still anymore and opened my legs. Even then she played me, said, "Come on and turn over."

I did what she said, turned onto my stomach and then felt her hand on my back, her mouth near my ear. I was rubbing myself against the bedspread and she kept doing the same things, touching my ass, the back of my thighs, and then she slipped onto me. Caught my wrists and held my arms over my head the way he had. And still she kept her mouth close to my ear, though she didn't say anything and neither did I.

I heard him before I felt him. Heard him pick up the chair and put it down again. He pulled my legs apart, just held them open.

She still wasn't saying anything and she wasn't doing anything but holding me, using all her weight, as if she needed to. He started to touch me. He used just one of his fingers and so slow and soft I nearly bit into my arm.

He did this a long while before he stopped. I heard him light a cigarette. Heard him take several draws before touching me again. And when he did, he rested the hand with the cigarette on my ass.

By now I either wanted to get off or get up. Had gone from being lulled to uncomfortable. He took his hand off me and I forgot myself. Moved to shake her off me.

Suddenly I felt her fear. And I felt him pressing his dick into my ass. The weight of him pushing her onto me. And that hand with the cigarette wasn't on my ass anymore.

She let go of my wrists and cuddled into me like a child. Whimpered like one too. And I thought, Son of a bitch.

Then the way she moved—shuddering first, then going rigid. I could smell the burn. I could almost hear it. The worst was she didn't make a sound. Just whimpered close to my ear.

He let her off me. And it left me with him. With him fucking my ass and her curled up into herself right beside us. I turned my head away from her because he let me.

I thought, I'll be leaving here soon.

Four

Afterward, he left us alone. We both watched the door, listened as he walked down the stairs. I don't think I wanted to look but I couldn't stop myself. It seemed necessary. That otherwise I'd make it up worse than it was. I held her nearly the way he'd held me and looked at her asshole.

The burn had already blistered but it looked almost tame. That's the thing with burns—they look best when they're new and then they get ugly.

I could tell she didn't like me looking and so I covered her with the bedspread. "Ingrid," I said a couple of times because she either wasn't listening or couldn't hear me. I said it again. Said, "Ingrid, can I do something for you?"

She didn't answer me and I sure didn't know what she'd need. I needed a cigarette. I even picked one up and started to light it. But this seemed in bad taste so instead I paced around. Wound up back looking at the pool.

It was a while before I started putting my clothes on. I even put on my shirt, though it felt clammy, still damp with his come. After I dressed, I left her. Closed the door quietly behind me and lit a cigarette as soon as I hit the staircase.

I found him on the living room couch. He lifted his glass toward another on the end table beside him. I picked up the drink, but stayed standing because I didn't want to be next to him and the only other place to sit was the floor.

This meant he got up. He took my cigarette, explaining he'd left his pack upstairs.

My bag was on the floor by the couch and I thought very hard about picking it up, finding a phone, calling a cab. These were things I knew I should do but wouldn't. And it didn't have to do with him or his wife but rather with where I'd be telling a cab driver to take me. Here with them was still somehow better than there in my parents' house by myself.

"You must be tired," he said. "I'll show you your room."

And so I picked up my bag and followed him back up the stairs. Their door was still closed. I kept staring at it as we turned down the hall, which was lit dimly with sconces, some of them bent and missing bulbs.

The second door on the right was the one he opened. His daughter's room. Big surprise. I hoped he wasn't planning a visit in the night. I didn't know what I should be charging, and if that was thrown in? Always with him I'd had trouble, but as soon as I'd stepped into his house, running the game wasn't even imaginable.

He flicked on the light in the bathroom, made sure there were towels, practically turned down the bed before he went out again. As soon as he had, I ducked out and went the rest of the way down the hall. I found a back stairway and then walked through the downstairs to the liquor cabinet.

I considered taking a whole bottle, but settled on pouring a tall glass of vodka. If this were to go on too much longer I knew I'd need more than liquor. But then, too, I knew he'd get it for me. Do it without my even having to ask.

I managed to drink myself to sleep on that one glass. Woke up the next morning when Ingrid brought coffee. I didn't inquire about her husband. I could tell by her hands, her steady grip on the tray, that he wasn't home.

She handed me the tray and climbed in beside me. I handed it back, and she fixed my coffee.

Daylight came in through a window behind us and I could see she was older than I'd thought, closer to his age, and I wondered how many years they'd been at this. Whether I was the beginning of something, or the end of it. I always come at one end or the other for people, never in the middle.

She'd curled up beside me and I put my arm around her and she put hers around me but on top of the sheet. She was wearing that negligee from the other night but with nothing else underneath it. I didn't have anything on and so when she held on to me I found I had to put down my cup.

This simple thing of her holding on suddenly frightened me because I couldn't get up from it. I couldn't walk away from it, not at first.

And I didn't know where it took Ingrid. I only knew she didn't try to move. She stayed quietly wrapped around me while I petted her. Finally what got me up and walking was my wanting to change this, my need to turn it into something it wasn't, and getting away from her was the only way to keep myself from doing this.

She didn't stop me or even say anything. I went into the bathroom, closed the door behind me and locked it just to prove I could. I washed my face, searched out a toothbrush and brushed my teeth. These were things I hadn't even attempted last night and so I was thorough about all of it. I considered taking a shower and realized my hesitation was fearing Ingrid wouldn't wait for me. Needing to feel clean won out.

I emerged wrapped in towels. She still lounged on the bed, watched me cross the room and get my bag, watched me take out the clothes I'd packed. I looked at them, but didn't want to put them on—a blouse and a skirt, garters and stockings. Another version of last night.

Ingrid said, "Over in the bureau there—my daughter's things. Go on."

I did what she suggested, and began rummaging through their girl's things. I found jeans in her bottom drawer, an old soft button-down in her closet, probably her father's castoff. Even her shoes fit. I tried not to think about how many ways we might resemble each other or what it might mean.

Ingrid watched me dress before she got up to leave. At the door, she told me she'd be downstairs in a little while and would I wait for her there?

I nodded and then listened to her footsteps, listened until I heard a door open and close and then listened some more to be sure before I sneaked down the back way. I took this route because I wanted to stay away from the living room. I wandered everywhere else you could go and still stay indoors. Covered the kitchen, the dining room, the little bar where I'd gotten last night's vodka.

At last I found a quiet room off the marble hall. If I left the door open, I could see the stairway and so I picked this place to wait. I opened the double doors to a terrace and then settled into a love seat—a comfortable one, not one for show.

I decided this was Ingrid's room, one her husband never bothered with. I was lost in this thought when I heard her on the stairs and then saw her.

She looked happier dressed this way—pants and a turtleneck sweater, her hair gathered loosely, her face a little easier without makeup.

I guess she probably thought the same things about me because she sort of smiled and held out her hand. I took it and floated to my feet, became caught up in her motion as she swept us out the door, took us outside.

We meandered over to the pool. "It's getting late in the year for this," she said, kneeling to scoop out some leaves. "I should call the man and have it drained."

I agreed with her but was wondering what I'd watch from the bedroom window if this was done.

We walked the rest of the grounds, through a withered garden and a little orchard of some kind. She talked about things she needed to do, about getting screens taken off and storm windows put on. She talked about where in the cellar to store things.

I stayed game for this, volunteered what I could about windows, and storage, and methods of leaf removal. Things I didn't know much about but that had occupied my parents at times, my mother, and so I could at least talk some of it, knew the words to use.

We went inside after a little more of this. She fed me in the kitchen. I sat at the counter eating eggs while she made some phone calls and then a shopping list. And then we were on our way to the supermarket, and then home again, and I was carrying the grocery bags for her.

By early afternoon we'd finished with these things. She made us large drinks and we sat by the pool in two big wooden lounge chairs, the only furniture still left out there.

We covered ourselves with afghans and just sat there drinking until she gauged it was time to go inside again. This was about two drinks later and so I followed her lead on wobbly legs. Had to hold the bannister all the way up the stairs.

We separated at her bedroom door—her going in, me going back to the daughter's room. There I put on my own clothes, did my hair, did the rest of it.

I was downstairs when he came home, sitting in the living room, sitting on that couch, which still had no table before it. As he opened the front door, I hitched up my skirt and opened my legs a little, lit a cigarette.

He stood in the hallway. Put his briefcase on the marble in a way that made a scraping sound. He fixed two drinks and I nearly reached for one but he took them upstairs. I heard voices, then other sounds. I waited while their noises grew louder, loud enough to send me back out to the pool.

Quiet out there. Wind and rustling, nothing human. I sat in one of the lounge chairs, cold without an afghan, cold anyway. Smoking, I pretended not to notice the shake in my hands, though before long I needed to go and get my own drink to stop it.

His briefcase still sat there in the hall. I watched it on my way to the bar. And I watched it when I walked to the little sitting room I'd pretended belonged to Ingrid. By now I could pretty much see nothing here belonged to her.

The sounds had stopped and so I listened hard to try and get my bearings. I heard nothing. I waited a long time and still heard nothing. I'd finished my drink some time ago and so poured another one before going upstairs.

I took the back route. Made my way down the hall, turned the door handle silently when I came to my room. I didn't turn on the light, not even in the bathroom. I laid my clothes on a chair and slipped into the bed.

First I heard the ice in his glass. The sound came from a corner by a bookshelf. It startled me even though I'd known he was there. I'd known while I roamed around downstairs. Known as soon as the sounds stopped. And so now I had the sense of having kept him waiting, of having done something wrong.

It'd been a while since I'd had a cigarette and so I took the pack from the bedside table. There wasn't a light anywhere nearby so I waited for him. He came across the room and sat on the edge of the bed. Lit my cigarette with a match and then kept the match burning, held it close to my cheek.

I tried just to smoke as if he wasn't doing this. It didn't hurt. It more felt awkward—the heat from it and him so close and still. And him staying that way until the match snuffed itself out between his fingers.

He put the shriveled remnant on the nightstand. I wanted to look at the pool but couldn't see it from this room and then, too, moving at all seemed like a very bad idea.

He didn't do anything but sit there and I didn't either. My cigarette had burned down and there was nowhere to put the ashes. I let them fall in the bed like I didn't notice. He finally took the still-lit nub from me and this scared me, but he just put it on the table next to what was left of the match. Not laying it on its side but upending it.

After this he got up, took his drink from the bedside table and left. I felt someway cheated. Like now I'd have to spend the night sleeping badly, wondering whether he'd be back, what else he'd want.

I searched for my drink, finally finding it on the bathroom sink. I drained it without thinking how I'd get more, what that would involve or invite. I wasn't up to foraging downstairs and so I tried to convince myself that this one would be enough to put me to sleep.

Five

He didn't come back, and the next morning Ingrid came in with the same tray. I drank the coffee she fixed me, knowing I couldn't spend another day with her running errands and talking about the screens and the pool, another day with her expecting me to play her daughter.

She looked like maybe she couldn't either. This morning she sat a little apart from me, concentrated on drinking her coffee and had trouble looking my way.

I put down my cup when I'd finished. Then I took her hand, the one next to me, which was empty. Her other hand was still holding her cup. It shook a little, sort of trembled, and so did her lips. The next sip she took, she spilled some coffee onto her nightgown.

I pretended not to see this and I think she really didn't notice. I began to worry what he'd done to her, but at the same time I knew it wasn't anything so very different. What it was, was her running out of ways to let herself take it. Running out of ways to make it her own, make it something she wanted.

Maybe. Or maybe this was only happening inside me and I wished it on her because together we might make something from feeling these things.

When she put down her cup, I kept hold of her hand. I kissed the crook of her elbow, licked the hollow there. She tensed, not just her arm, but her whole body. And because of this I got on top of her.

I pulled her down under me. Held her face in my hands and looked at her until I couldn't anymore. I began kissing her for an excuse to close my eyes.

From there it got easier. I pulled her nightgown up a little and then took it off her entirely. Once I'd done that I felt her sink into the bed more. She opened her legs and then put her hand between my legs, began to play me in such a way I rolled off her, lay on my back and just let her.

She kissed my stomach and worked her hand and that was all of it. All she did, and when I came it seemed like something I hadn't done in a very long time. She kept at me afterward, kept teasing me until I took her wrist, pressed it into the bed and then rolled back onto her, leaned all my weight into her.

I caught where I was headed and turned gentler. She liked this at first. Wanted me kissing her neck, wanted me stroking her the way she'd stroked me. So I kept at this. Slow and soft. Ignored the way she began moving her hips, the way she'd opened her legs. Ignored it until she wouldn't let me anymore and was asking.

When I fucked her, I started out that same kind of slow and easy but she was asking for it hard. And then it wasn't so long before she pulled away from me.

I let my hand come out, let her turn over. I knew what she wanted me to do. And knew I'd be no good to her if I couldn't manage it. I started playing with her ass. I could tell she was impatient. I tried to pretend, at least to myself, that I had a reason for this. Did it to up the ante. But the change in pace made this unconvincing, and made her anxious.

I could feel the roughness of the burn where it'd healed over, felt her tense as I touched it. I couldn't be so cruel as to make her ask and so I just did it. Did it as bluntly as she wanted. Did it until she was crying and pulling my other hand under her, but insisting I keep fucking her.

Finally when she'd had enough, when she'd come, she pulled away from me. She drew herself up into the corner of the bed, curled up and unapproachable. So much so I wondered whether I should leave the room. And then I nearly did, but felt too guilty to, until she demanded it.

I pulled on the jeans and shirt I'd worn yesterday and then got out of there. I took the main stairs and then went through the living room, out to the pool. I sat in the chair that was becoming home and tried to find reasons for what I was feeling.

I hated how clearheaded I was, how sober. I would've made for a drink except it would've meant going inside—something I'd decided I wouldn't do until she asked for me.

I wanted to leave her completely alone. I knew I'd indulged myself, and not her, by lingering. By making her kick me out while pretending she'd need me or want me.

I understood what had happened between us. Or to her. I knew it, though I couldn't explain it, or maybe just wouldn't, not even to myself. I knew it from her side, hated how helpless and feeble I'd become. I could only imagine she felt contempt for me because that's what I felt for myself.

It took me this long to notice how cold I was, and then longer to see there was nothing anywhere out here that'd help. I hugged myself, rubbed my hands over my shoulders until I could imagine this warmed me. I got lost really, just in how my own hands soothed me. Soon I closed my eyes and soon after I let go of myself and tried to ignore it when I began shaking again.

She finally did come outside and sit with me. She wore a big sweater that looked like the kind someone knits for you. She noticed my shivering and held out her arms and so I clambered into her chair with her, let her wrap us up together and I think then I slept or did something close to it. I don't know what she did or how long this lasted.

That night worked differently. Because of us really, her and me. We'd gone from the chair by the pool to her bed. I hadn't been in there since that one night. We'd moved inside because we were cold and cramped. We'd gone upstairs to be comfortable, gone to her room because it was closest. This was the kind of day we were having. Nothing registered except wanting comfort.

We lay on the bed. On top of it, with our clothes on, her in that sweater still. We pulled a quilt over us because it seemed we couldn't get warm enough and then we drifted some more. Drifted somewhere else, or maybe back to the same place, I don't know.

It seemed he never came home. That's how it seemed at first. Then she noticed cufflinks right there on the table beside us. And I saw the suit coat draped on a chair and a tie neatly folded over it. Then I guess we drifted off again because we never did see him, just saw his things.

This started something ticking in me. Started me wondering and I could tell she was wondering too but it was too soon to say anything. I think we were afraid of ourselves. Afraid of what we'd accomplished by accident. What we'd managed out of fatigue and soreness.

For this reason we worked the next day differently. We kept away from each other. She took the car off somewhere. Completely alone for the first time in days I'd stopped counting, I weighed leaving altogether. I could've left in the sense I was able to. No one would stop me. But that was because no one needed to.

I pretended to consider it—as if to prove to myself I could. That staying was a choice I was making for money. Money I had yet to see. In truth, leaving had become inconceivable. And, worse, I couldn't tell for sure which one of them held me.

When she came home, late in the afternoon, both of us dressed for him. Me in another version of the same thing, her in another negligee.

I was ready before she was so I stood in the doorway of her bedroom and watched her. Then we went downstairs to wait. Sat on the couch in the living room—me smoking and drinking, her just drinking.

He was late. We both noticed and it made us jumpy and hopeful. We were giddy, nearly, by the time we heard his car on the gravel, and then his key, and the door, his briefcase on the marble.

He fixed himself a drink and sat across from us. "What have the two of you been up to?" he asked. These might have been the first words I'd heard out loud all day. I searched my brain trying to remember whether Ingrid had said anything today, or even yesterday. Whether I had.

"We've been idle," she said, and her voice scared me like I was losing her and me both to her words.

"Is that true?" he said to me.

"I suppose so."

I said this not quite sure I was speaking, not sure what he wanted to hear.

"That's good then," he said. "You're rested."

I tried to figure what this meant. Whether we'd made some kind of mistake. I'd forgotten for a minute that what we said didn't matter.

He said, "Here, Ingrid. Fix me another."

She went and took his glass, crossed the room to the bar. He got up himself and sat beside me. He said, "I have something special, something just for you." He put his arm around my shoulders. With his other hand he dropped a pill into my mouth. And then he began stroking my throat like you would an animal. I tipped my head back into the crook of his arm. Heard him whisper to me that I'd like it.

At first, I felt nothing at all, but soon I'd slumped against him. I could barely see Ingrid coming back with his drink, then felt her sit down on the other side of me. I closed my eyes, though this seemed foolish. His hand had gone from my throat to my chest. He opened buttons, began undressing me. I felt her hands in this, too, until I had nothing on.

In my mind I kept struggling, not against them but to figure out what he'd given me. I couldn't imagine what had knocked me so far and done it so fast.

He carried me upstairs but Ingrid didn't come with us. I hadn't heard him tell her to stay. It seemed she just knew to.

When he put me down on their bed I reached for the bedspread. I wanted to cover myself with it. I felt cold and less groggy because of this. He smacked me hard enough that I lay still, then he took off his belt, doubled it over and hit me a few times. Across the face mostly, and my breasts, but with the drug it felt like an afterthought.

He looped it around my neck and cinched it through the buckle, tied my hands together with the end. Pretty soon after that I woke up for real. The goddamn drug wasn't there anymore and I had him on my chest and taking his dick out. He rubbed it against my cheek until it was hard. Then he slid down me.

"You're going to like this," he said. Said it like he knew everything about me better than I did. His hands were between my legs opening me up and then putting his dick in. He fucked me slow at first like to make sure where I was, to make sure I was feeling things.

I paid attention to my arms. With my hands tied that way I could only move them so much before I choked myself. I had to keep them over my head but bent in a way that started to ache very quickly.

He could see how hard I had to work at this—was all over his face. That slight smile I'd come to expect. He had his arms on either side of me. They took his weight so he could hold himself over me. I wanted anything but him watching me so close, felt this pull to close my eyes but as soon as I did he took hold of my arms. Pushed them until I was strangling myself. Or he was.

This meant I couldn't scream but then I don't think I tried to. I think maybe I cried, though I'm not sure of it. I know what he did lasted a long time. That he fucked me a long time before he pulled out. That he was still hard when he went back to sitting on my chest and telling me to open my mouth. Smacking me when I didn't, but not very hard because he didn't need to.

I didn't do so well at sucking him. His belt still choked me and his dick did too—made him impossible to swallow. He seemed to like that, though. That seemed to be the point because he let himself come until I was choking all over myself.

After this he got off me. Zipped himself up. He still had his shoes on and his socks, and when he ran his fingers through his hair, smoothing it back, the glint from one of his cufflinks stayed caught in my eye.

He hadn't even had to roll up his sleeves, and from this I thought about Ingrid the other night in the bathtub and how I couldn't quite understand her. Him still in his cufflinks persuaded me that'd been a lie. That I knew exactly and had known it then. Only I hadn't wanted to admit it and I was beginning to see how this sort of refusal on my part—this unwillingness to admit to things stronger than me—didn't keep me from trouble but kept leading me to it.

Six

I lay there and waited. He'd left the room, left me tied, and I couldn't undo the knot so I waited.

I didn't sleep. The pull to close my eyes wasn't there anymore now that I needed it. The belt was thin so it cut into my neck and my wrists. Now and then I tried halfheartedly to untie myself, knowing I couldn't and that it hurt to try.

I wanted Ingrid to come get me and at the same time the last thing I wanted was for her to see me this way—lying here still naked and still tied, and with his come all over my face and my neck and my chest. I don't know what I thought it said about me. I think I was more concerned with what it said about her. Not wanting to show her herself, which maybe was also part of his game. Making her be the one to clean up after him.

I heard nothing from downstairs. Nothing at all. I could've gotten up. It's not like he'd tied my legs. But they still wouldn't move. Like that part of me slept while the rest of me stayed wide awake.

My chest heaved as if still carrying his weight. My shoulders ached. But my wrists and neck hurt more and different. I traded them off. Rested my shoulders until I couldn't stand it and had to rest my neck instead.

Ingrid did come in. She turned the light out as soon as she saw me, and which of us she was sparing, I couldn't know. For a moment when she sat down near me I feared her terribly. Feared her more than him. And when she touched my hands, moving them to get at his knot, I jerked away. I made a sound I didn't recognize. A whimpering I didn't believe could come from my body.

She quieted me. She stroked my arms until they rested, making some slack for her to work with. Once she had the knot undone, she slipped the shank through the buckle. Then she lifted my head a little to slide the belt away.

"Don't," I said when she started to get up.

"I'll just be a minute. You'll see."

I watched her move across the room to the bathroom. She didn't turn on the light in there either. I heard water running for a while and then she came back. Brought two towels, one of them wet.

She cleaned him off me, then she got more towels, some of these were wet too. She slipped one under my neck. The dampness took some sting from the cuts there. She wrapped another towel around my wrists. I rested my hands in my lap, liking how the coolness felt there, opening my legs to it, and she laid another towel across my thighs. She did all of this like she'd done it before—something I couldn't let myself think about.

When she finished all this, I faded in and out. Woke once to her smoking a cigarette. When she saw I was awake she held it for me so I could have some. After that I slept the night.

I woke up achy. She'd taken away the towels but the pillow behind me was damp. I put my arms up to try and flip it over but they wouldn't move in that way. Instead I slid over to her side. I wanted more blankets because I couldn't get warm.

I was glad she wasn't there but didn't want her to have left entirely. I didn't want to be thinking about him, but I was. I was trying to figure out what made last night any different. Whether the difference was in him or in me because this seemed to matter. It was something I wanted to ask her but I knew we'd never talk this way.

Later she brought coffee just like she had those other mornings, though it all seemed wrong in this room. She helped me sit up because I couldn't do this alone and I began worrying what else I couldn't do.

"He won't be back for a while," she said, handing me a cup. "What do you take in it? I can't remember."

This hurt my feelings and so I didn't answer her. She poured some cream. Left off the sugar as if she remembered after all but didn't want to admit it.

"You should leave while he's gone."

"I should," I said. And that's how it started.

She looked at me funny. Like no one had suggested this to her before or like she'd never thought it herself. Like she thought it all the time.

"Yes, you should," she said, like that would be the end of it. She started to get up. I grabbed her wrist and pulled her back hard. Everything on the tray beside us spilled.

"Leave it," I said when she started fussing. And when she didn't stop I grabbed it from her hands. Just barely kept myself from throwing it across the room.

The trouble was, it would've gotten through to her. It would've worked. And it troubled me too that my strength and clarity came from my anger at her, while I couldn't find any toward him. And realizing this made my body hurt again, or made me notice it still did.

I put the tray down on the floor and asked her, "Haven't you ever planned it?"

"Once," she said. "After our daughter ..." She stopped herself and then started again. "After she left. Don't you see he'd never let me?"

"I know."

"He'd find me."

"Maybe."

"You, though, you'd better get out."

I lit a cigarette. And then seeing her face, I gave it to her and lit another one. I said, "He still owes me money." I said this just to stall. I didn't want to leave. I couldn't imagine leaving.

"I'll pay you. I'll pay you right now if that's what matters."

She started to get up again. I didn't grab her this time. I said, "No, please stay with me."

We didn't talk about it anymore that day and I made no move to leave. We puttered around, not doing anything. She still hadn't taken care of the screens or the pool. We wandered around out there but she said nothing about these things. Late in the afternoon we took a drive together.

It seemed we hadn't been out in such a long time. I was surprised at how easy it was. I kept half expecting someone to stop us, a cop to pull us over and send us home, or maybe men wearing overcoats and hats, driving a sedan.

"We could just drive away," I said because it had occurred to me.

She looked at me like she wished this were true and knew it wasn't. Like this was the fanciful idea of a child. I felt like one, then acted like one by pouting.

"You're very sweet," she said.

I liked that she said this, but when she reached her hand toward me I cowered, huddled against the door and stayed that way a long time.

I couldn't understand how I'd gotten to this place. We drove and drove, never once stopping anywhere. Finally she turned the car around and we went back.

We ate what we could find in the refrigerator and then went up to her bed. When it was dark I said, "Is that what the others did? Left the first chance they got?"

She didn't answer me but I could see her nodding.

"Your daughter, too?"

She began to cry when I asked this, but what she said was, "Don't you see, you have to leave? That this only makes it worse?"

"How?"

"He'll expect you to be gone. He'll get someone else."

"Why are you doing this?"

"What am I doing? I'm living my life. You're the one who wants to die."

"What are you talking about?"

"Why can't you just leave?"

"I'm asking you the same thing."

"And I've told you."

And I suppose to shut me up she began kissing me. At first I didn't want her to. It felt wrong. But soon she'd gone far enough I didn't care how it started. Only cared how it felt and about letting her finish me.

Once she'd done this it felt wrong again. And I felt wrong and sad. But this seemed all inside me. Like it had nothing to do with her anymore.

I started in on her only to get away from my loneliness. Soon this began working. Working just as well as what she'd done to me.

And I could feed off her sounds and her movements, could feed off her wanting me. I got very far away on this. And so when she'd finished, or when I'd finished her, it could almost seem like this was the only thing there'd ever been between us. And that all we'd ever really needed or wanted was sleep.

Seven

We left each other alone about it for another day or so. Then we started planning. She began it. Out of nowhere she said, "We could go together."

She said we'd have to put distance between him and us. At first we'd need to and then it might be safest to come back. Not here but nearby. Be far enough he wouldn't run into us, near enough he wouldn't think to look.

The way she said these things I could see she'd planned it over and over. Had every detail worked out. That she'd even planned it for two and that's when I thought of the daughter. Worried this was why she said we should come back this way instead of going farther away. Worried about this another day before asking her.

"No, that isn't it," she insisted with an absoluteness I believed, deciding the daughter's school must be in Switzerland, somewhere that far away. But then I worried that's where the husband went. Maybe even where he was right now. And I shouldn't have asked her but I couldn't not.

She said, "You think I'd allow that? Is that what you think of me?"

"What do you care what I think? Look where he found me."

We left it there. I think both of us felt badly about ourselves. I did anyway. I knew I had to quit pressing the daughter thing. But because I was trying not to, I kept tripping over it. Finding things to ask about, and not being able to stop myself until one night we were sitting on the couch having drinks and I asked how old she was. I said, "How old is your daughter?"

Ingrid stared past me, not through me. Already I knew. I knew I'd known all along. And I wished I could take back every stupid question I'd asked her.

"Sixteen," she said, "always sixteen. Do you understand now? Will you leave it alone?"

I didn't say anything at first. I didn't do anything. She went for another drink. When she sat down with it she asked me for a cigarette. I handed her one and lit it for her.

"How long ago?" I asked because to my mind this was a practical question—something I needed to know.

"Five years."

She still stared off somewhere. I knew she'd tell me whatever I wanted to know if I could stand prodding her. I wanted to know all of it. I told myself I needed to, and so I began asking. "On purpose?" I said.

"No, no. He got carried away. That never describes him very well but that is what happened."

"You were there?" I asked. I could hear the fear in my voice. The fear that she'd stood by and watched.

"I came home to him on the couch, sitting where you are. He told me to go up and look in on her. I found her just as I found you the other night.

"We called the police. He did. He called someone he knew. A report was written, describing an accident. I don't know that he ever thinks about it except for bringing home you girls. I don't know that that means he thinks about it."

"You think about it."

"Yes, I do," she said. And she looked at me for the first time since we began this.

We went up to her bed again, but already everything between us was different. Our tiredness had been gauzy before but now it had a sharpness to it, like we knew where it came from. We lay down together, not touching at first. The lights were out, making the room seem smaller first and then bigger—a place you could get lost in.

I got up and went to the bathroom. Really just wanted somewhere else to be for a minute. Wanted to be without her, though I couldn't tolerate this for very long.

On my way back I looked out at the pool. I stopped, stood still but the lights weren't on tonight. Just blackness out there. When I got in the bed I held on to her. I didn't know what to do except touch her. But I couldn't be sure what she wanted. Whether she wanted this.

Soon I could tell from her body. It went loose in a way I'd never felt before. She became truly easy instead of resigned. Something about this softness made me soft. And I did everything slowly and stayed gentle. Stroked her and kissed her this way.

She was on her back and I spent a long time just touching her, her arms and her shoulders, her stomach. And after a while she began telling me things that couldn't possibly be true but which I wanted to hear. Things I'd always wanted to hear. She told me I meant something to her. That I'd made a difference, had changed something for her.

I drew myself alongside her, kissed her mouth in a way I hadn't before. She pulled me closer and held on and I held on too until I couldn't. Then I slid her onto her back more, pressed my body into hers and began to rub against her. And even though this wasn't about that, I made it into that. Was soon kissing her the way I usually did and opening her legs and trying very hard to make this just any other time.

She let me. Maybe she even helped me because after a while she'd turned onto her stomach. Was asking me to fuck her. Once this started she wanted it harder and I did what she said. I was wanting it this way myself but not wanting to be giving it this way. I didn't think so. But I couldn't be sure because I'd gotten caught up in her movement. The way she lifted her hips and then slumped down again. The sounds she was making. But when she asked me to hit her I stopped.

It wasn't something we'd done before. And I didn't think I could. Not even with her needing me to. We'd come halfway around and then some. We were so far from where we'd started I didn't think we'd ever get back there. And I was afraid the only way back might be to do what she asked. And then, too, I figured the only reason I craved that softness again was how hard this was getting. And I didn't think I'd like feeling tender once we got there. I thought instead it would bust me all up.

It was already too late. I'd left her out there alone and she turned away from me. Drew her knees to her chest and lay there not making a sound. I knew whatever I did now, soft or hard, would be forced. She was that unapproachable.

What I did was get up. I left her alone because I'd already done that. And I walked downstairs knowing I'd failed her. That I'd pushed her toward wanting something and then left her alone wanting it. Who was I to decide what was good for her? Though really that hadn't had anything to do with it. Really, I was afraid. And I couldn't be sure where the fear came from and this was the trouble. Except this wasn't true either. What I might've done to her was the trouble. That I might've been too good at what she asked of me.

I spent the rest of the night on the couch. Curled up under that same afghan we'd used out by the pool. I didn't sleep exactly. I kept floating in and out, and when I heard her come into the room I didn't know what to expect so I played I was sleeping. She pulled the blanket up around me, sat beside me, petting me, and it was like last night hadn't happened.

I could almost believe this until I wanted to get up, wanted to put clothes on and realized I couldn't wear the ones I'd been wearing anymore. Then I looked at her differently—the way I had yesterday.

She didn't seem to notice or maybe she did because she began telling me things. Saying stuff like she had last night, stuff about having feelings for me. This is where I got scared. Not because I knew not to believe her, but because I wanted so much for her to say these things whether they were true or not. I knew how close this brought me to getting caught up in her make-believe, and so I began right then to ask when he'd be home.

I thought this would keep me safe from both of them and so I kept asking. But when I did, she held out her arms and I went to her. I let her hold me and pet me. She told me not to worry, that we'd be gone by then. With her talking this way and her touching, I landed right where I'd started. And so I stopped asking and started guessing.

I'd lost all sense of time. Had no way to know how long he'd been gone—a week, maybe ten days. I didn't believe he'd stay away much longer than this, but how could I know? Clearly he didn't expect me to still be here. Clearly she knew what to expect.

More and more I began to let her take over. But always nagging me were the questions I hadn't asked her. These came down to "How did you let him?" which seemed to make it more her fault than his but I really wasn't driving at blame. It still seemed practical. Like I needed to know if I could rely on her. If I could at all.

And so I began to ask her again, ask her when he'd be back. Until one evening, not too long after, when we were lying together in much the same way, I pressed it too hard. She let go of me. She got up and walked. Then she turned on me. She said, "You want him back. You miss him."

She said it like it just dawned on her. But it hadn't yet come to me. Hadn't occurred to me that maybe I did need him. That it was simpler with him there. That the sort of jeopardy she put me in was worse. And because of this, because I could see she might just be right, I said, "No, I don't. I worry about it, that's all."

"I don't think so," she said. "You forget I've seen you with him. I've seen how you get."

"What are you talking about?"

"You'd do anything."

Now I was angry, swallowing tears but with nothing to say.

"You pretend it's about money. That without the money, you'd never have come here. That it makes you different than me …"

"It is why I came."

"Oh, please. You can't for a minute believe that, so how are you to convince me?"

Her saying this put me back to that first time with him in that parking lot. Even approaching me he'd been different. He walked straight up to me and said, "You looking for something?" Then he'd laughed and said, "My car's over there." And when I didn't immediately follow, he took my arm. Said, "Let's go, honey." Already, he had me thinking it'd be easier this way. That always running the game had begun tiring me, and so why not let him do it?

Eight

I spent that night back in their daughter's room. I thought I'd be the one to leave. That I'd leave the next morning. Make way for whoever came next. I never thought she'd leave but that's what happened. She actually went and did it. And I'd slept through it. So now I figured I had to get out and fast. Had to hope he wouldn't connect her leaving to me.

I didn't have much money. The same few hundred he'd given me before all this started. I considered rummaging through things, trying to find more. I thought I shouldn't go back to my parents' house. That there was a chance he'd come looking. Four hundred dollars would get me just about nowhere.

I guessed there'd be a little window. That she hadn't been planning to leave yet and so he wouldn't be back right away. I called a cab and went home. I was surprised at how easy it was. I couldn't shake the worry, though, even when I'd showered and was finally dressed in my own jeans and shirt. When I was sitting on the couch in my parents' living room, drinking their booze and not his, even then I kept expecting someone to stop me.

I stayed pretty much in the house. Just went out to shop for food, things like that. My nerves settled pretty soon, and good thing because the money was running low. I actually thought about getting my old job back. I really did, for a minute or so, before I decided I needed to get some cash in before I could consider that sort of thing.

I realize going back to the parking lot does not seem like the best thing or the smartest. But I'd begun to feel easy. I thought that because I was out of his house that'd be the end of it. That he couldn't reach me, wouldn't bother. I even thought I could go back to doing him in his car. That it'd make sense because he wanted more and so paid more. I not only thought all this stuff, I came to believe it.

So I began working the commuters again. And it seemed I was right because I didn't see any sign of him. The old regulars acted glad to see me and so I upped my rate a little. Began making more for less off these guys. Began to appreciate them again, and then began to get bored.

One evening, I saw someone new on the platform. He craned his neck like he was looking for his wife picking him up. I'd all but pictured the station wagon and the dog in the back when he began heading my way.

Coming up to me he said, "I hear you're worth it."

I was thinking, this isn't how they usually talk. I said, "That depends. What is it you're wanting?"

He said, "Let's talk in my car."

It was already dark and a pretty cold night, so this seemed like a good idea, or at least not a bad one. We crossed the lot, all the way to the other end. His was the only car left that far over, a four-door green sedan. One look and I knew. It was that kind of car.

He had hold of my arm.

I said, "Hey, look, I don't think so. Not tonight."

Who was I kidding?

I could see his partner in the backseat waiting. He was the one who shoved the door open. Then the one behind me was pushing and this one was yanking, and then he cuffed me. Looped one end through one of those metal door-handle things, the kind cabs sometimes have. I noticed because my head hit it, though even before that I was dazed. So much so it took me a bit to realize where I'd wound up. It took feeling hands in my hair, fingers running through it, and then I turned my head in his lap, could feel the other one still behind me and pushing.

I had one knee on the seat, curled up under me, the other on the floor. And the guy behind me wasn't pushing anymore, but pulling instead. Pulling at my clothes until he had everything off me but my shirt.

The other guy was too busy with his own clothes to bother with mine. He'd spent these few moments getting his dick out and into my mouth. He didn't say a word, just held me against his lap in a way that hurt my neck. And with my head turned this way it was hard to do what he wanted, hard to take him.

The other one was the talker. He said, "I heard you like it in the ass. Am I right?" And he was nudging me there, pulling me apart with his hands and stroking me. "Guess so," he said, laughing. I could feel how slippery I was and then felt his dick rubbing me.

When he put it in, it hurt because he stayed slow about it, kept right at that place where the pain stays bad because you can't ease up and you can't ease up because of the pain. I knew he was staying there on purpose. Normally I guess I would've chewed on something but the other guy in my mouth made that not a good option and so finally I couldn't hold still for it.

I jerked, my whole body did. And the way I moved my head

and my mouth brought the one guy off, but I guess he wasn't ready because he pulled his dick away fast and was cursing me. I don't know, maybe I hurt him. I could tell he wanted out of the car. But so did I.

I was still trying to swallow him. And the guy behind me was making this harder. He had his hand on my neck and was pressing. Pressing me into the other one's thigh. And then, still staying in that same place in my ass, he started dicking around. Moving in and out and so I was swallowing more and more until I pulled my arms down. Did this so the cuffs would eat into my wrists and it helped, it got me quieter.

He got quieter too. Quiet in a way that made me figure he'd forgotten me and remembered himself. When I felt him move the rest of the way in, that's when I nearly cried. From the relief of it. I let up on my arms and sank into the other one's lap, wanted his hands in my hair again.

The one behind me, he'd put his hands underneath me. Was almost holding me. He had his hand on my stomach and I felt myself rocking back into him. Could feel his other hand between my legs, his fingers playing me.

He kept at this pretty long and so I could stay lost in the movements of his hands. But then he came and once that happened he pulled out quick like the other one had. Told him to unlock me. The guy couldn't wait to, he did it fast. Was already on his way out of the car and that left just me and the talker.

He cuffed me again, this time with my hands behind my back. "You're pretty," he said, and he unbuttoned my shirt, unhooked my bra, and for a while he just looked. Then he put two fingers to my lips, forced them into my mouth. He traced down my chin and my throat, my breasts. First one, then the other.

"All of you's pretty," he said, opening my legs. He seemed back to looking but then he stroked me and so now we both knew I was wet. "So you haven't had enough yet."

He said this putting his fingers into me, fucking me a little but then stopping. "Don't worry," he said, "you'll get plenty."

Then he was laughing again and I was back to pulling at the cuffs so they cut my wrists. And after some more of this laughing and looking he said, "Let's see. We've read you your rights."

I nodded because what did it matter?

"And, smart girl like you, you understand them."

I nodded again.

"All right then," he said. "Not much else to do." He opened the door, which he'd never quite closed. Got out and then leaned back in. He found my bag somewhere on the floor, and after a glance inside he threw it into the front seat. Then he picked my clothes off the floor and tossed them my way. Said, "Here, get yourself dressed." And then he was laughing again.

The two of them got in front. He did the driving. I just sat there. Leaned back hard against my arms because except for my wrists it didn't hurt to do this. And besides, the hurting wasn't so bad and leaning forward left me bumping around.

I braced myself with my feet, but without my shoes I didn't like how the floor felt—gritty and sticky in places and hot from the heater. The whole car felt this way, the seat against my skin felt sweaty and I wanted them to open a window. Still, the worst thing was knowing the drive wouldn't last long. That the police station wasn't more than a few blocks away.

Sure enough we got there soon. The quiet guy started in before the other one turned off the engine. Me, obviously I had to wait. He came around and opened the door, told me to get out. The asphalt was cold and I shifted my feet back and forth and couldn't help shivering. He took his coat off and put it around my shoulders. He didn't button it, though. He fished around the car until he found my clothes and my shoes again. Rolled all of it together and tucked the bundle under his arm with my bag. Then I felt his hand on my neck, steering me.

It wasn't one of those bustling station houses, just a small-town one. There weren't more than two or three cops there, them and a desk sergeant who sat at an actual desk, a small one, not some big embankment. He called my escort "Pete." Said, "What you got there, Pete?"

Pete said, "Just what it looks like."

You might think with less people around it'd be easier, standing there the way I was, but it made it worse because it meant the ones who were there looked and kept looking. Had nothing else to move on to and so lingered.

And it meant a man did the searching and him being older and embarrassed about it only made it harder. I would've rather Pete had done it, though at least this one got my skirt back. He let me put it on, and my shoes and my stockings, and let me button my shirt. I never did get my underwear back.

I was the only girl inside. And there were just two men in the adjoining cell, too drunk to notice me much after a small fanfare. I sat on the bench—the one that goes around the edge in that kind of cell, most of the way around anyway. I wanted to pace but stopped myself because of how it would look. And how it would feel, too. It'd get me worked up, only remind me more where I was.

Sitting, I could close my eyes and forget things—almost not be here or anywhere.

I wanted a cigarette. I had for a long time. But I knew it'd take me quite a while before I could manage asking for favors. I told myself I'd be able to if Pete wasn't there. Or if he was the only one there. I still had my eyes closed but I could hear him recounting my arrest for the others. They weren't saying anything, just grunted occasionally. Like the one who searched me, they seemed mostly embarrassed.

I couldn't tell if I was embarrassed. I didn't quite listen but I heard some of it and then some more. And then I opened my eyes. Pete was saying, "I got her in the car and that's when I showed her my badge and you know what she does? Huh? She unbuttons her shirt. She shows me her tits and tells me I can suck them. Starts grabbing at my belt and when that doesn't work, she takes off her skirt and the rest of it. Won't put her clothes back on. Just keeps showing herself to me. I had to cuff her to keep her still. Go on and ask Ed."

Ed wasn't around, not that I could see, and pretty soon Pete was gone too. That's when something inside me shifted. When I noticed he'd left, my breathing changed and I thought I might cry if I didn't get a cigarette. The desk sergeant gave me my pack. Lit one for me and then soon after he was lighting another, though already I'd begun rationing. Counting how many were left and how long they could last me.

The whole night went that way. Counting things. Hours, bars, cinder blocks—anything at all to keep from examining the exact way I'd gotten here. And just who'd had his hand in it.

Nine

The next day, first thing, Ed and Pete took me over to the county courthouse. They'd showered and changed. They'd probably even slept. I wore the same clothes.

They gave me ten minutes with my public defender. I spent most of it trying to make sure he couldn't see I wasn't wearing underwear. I concentrated on this because it was clear from the start I wouldn't be able to control anything else.

The guy said his name was Jim something. He started talking before he even sat down. He told me a concerned citizen had taken an interest. He actually used those words. Anyway, this concerned person had offered to foot the bill for my rehab.

"Rehab for what?" I said.

Jim looked at me like "get serious." Then he said, "It's a good deal. It keeps you a minor. That wouldn't be possible otherwise."

"So what," I said. "How long could they keep me?"

"They've got resisting arrest, attempted assault on an officer."

That sobered me some. Seemed getting fucked in the car was just the beginning of the fuckings lined up for me, that Ingrid's husband had lined up.

I should've realized this sooner except I wouldn't let myself think. Not for a minute. I couldn't believe he'd spend this kind of time and money on me. The arrest, yeah, well sure, but this? But then if he couldn't get to Ingrid, who else was there?

I glazed over. Let Jim lay it out for me. A private rehab facility. This was the deal that was supposed to excite me. Make me feel lucky. Spare me from sixty or ninety days locked up with the big girls.

"How long?" I asked, as if there were a choice anywhere in sight.

"That depends on your progress."

I wondered if Jim actually believed any of this. Hard to tell from the way he explained it. His voice cracked from overuse, but otherwise rolled out flat. I'd softened to him though because he seemed to be working just as hard not to look up my skirt as I was working to make it hard for him. This let me decide he wasn't part of the larger thing.

So there was an informal hearing, a closed one. The judge gave me a chance to talk. "Do you have anything to say for yourself?" was how he put it. I decided I didn't. The concerned citizen never appeared, though it seemed he'd also made the original complaint.

By four that afternoon I was being searched again, this time by a woman and more thoroughly. She gave me some different clothes to wear and then she locked me up by myself. Completely by myself. I figured I must've come with instructions.

I don't know how long this went on. How many days I spent alone in that room. I'd given up counting. Had left that idea back in the holding cell. They brought me food, they came by and lit cigarettes. They took me to the bathroom, but I had to ask and then they stood there and watched.

The room was too small to pace but I found myself doing it anyway. I didn't sleep really. I'd had an instant aversion to the mattress, which lay on the floor in one corner. I didn't like that it didn't have sheets, and it was that plasticky kind. But then maybe this made it harder to set on fire—something I'd already considered but hadn't attempted because it seemed almost expected. Mostly I didn't like that I couldn't see well. The room was too dim, all day and all night, the only light coming from the hallway.

I knew the time of day by what was on the food tray. Went by this until I got to where I could only eat toast. Then I tried to remember which woman worked which shift. A nice one followed by two mean ones and then the nice one again.

I knew that the nice one, Gail, had the day shift. But soon I found it easier to think of her as working the midnight to morning one. Even wished hard that it was true because that would've given her more time with me. The woman who really worked that shift sure had plenty to spare.

They kept Gail busy but she still spent time with me. She'd come in and sit with me on that mattress. She'd talk to me. She'd light my cigarettes as if she was just being friendly instead of reminding me I couldn't do it myself. Instead of getting me on my knees for it. And she never once forced me to eat. Coaxed me sometimes but she never tried to force me.

In this way it was good she worked days because it gave me two meals with her, and only dinner with the one who'd push, who'd get her arm around my neck and insist. These day-to-day things had begun running me.

Gail's the one who brought Beth to me. Sometimes I think if Gail hadn't I'd still be in that hole. You get to see pretty fast why people call it that. The darkness, and the way that makes the edges hard to make out.

Anyway, Gail brought Beth in there with me. And the first thing Beth did was put her arms around me. Even in that light I could see the look on her face.

I began to count again, to count days. And for five of them, including the first one, Beth came to that room. The sixth and seventh meant the weekend because she didn't come and Gail didn't come either. On Monday they both came again.

The day after that I went for my first walk. Beth took me. She actually took me outside. And I began to wonder where in my hell she'd come from because this small thing—taking me outside where I could breathe—seemed huge and important and nearly unreal and I couldn't see where she found the strength for it.

I quickly found I didn't have much strength. There were woods all around, the hilly kind. It seemed if you could run—if you were physically able, I mean, in a way I knew I wasn't—you could get lost fast. I hadn't seen any dogs or even guards but we hadn't exactly gone anywhere near the gates.

This sort of thing passed through my mind; it didn't really settle. If somewhere I was working on it, I didn't know because Beth claimed all my attention. She held my arm while we walked. Helped me up the little slopes.

I'd slept some this week. Slept lying on that mattress instead of crouched down in the corner trying to fight it off. Instead of trying to keep awake in the furthest corner as if that could protect me from the midnight-to-morning woman and who she'd bring with her. Who she might let in while she sat by the door, keeping watch and no doubt collecting on me.

These last nights I'd stretched out and slept. And when they came, I let them because I found this way I could pretend to be sleeping and it'd go faster. It'd seem to, and I'd get hit less. And I'd be thinking how the next day I'd see her. Beth. I'd be thinking for the first time that I might not always be here.

Beth seemed to be thinking this too. Seemed to have assumed it right from the start. The fourth day we went out walking she stopped and sat down, propped herself against a log that was lying there.

Still slow on the uptake, and not used to doing things unless told to, I just stood there. Loomed over her, and I'm sure I looked pretty empty. She grabbed my hand. Pulled me down next to her and ran her fingers through my hair.

She laughed at me in a way I liked. In a way that was nice to me. She put her arm around my shoulders and I leaned against her. Left off trying to bolster myself, left this to her.

"How did you wind up in there?" she asked first. And still thinking small scale, I assumed she meant the room.

"I don't know," I said. "Practically the minute I got here, that's where they put me."

"But how did you get here?"

I thought she would know all this. I said, "You're the one who works here. Don't they tell you that stuff? Isn't it all written down?"

I'd leaned away a little when I said this. I wanted enough distance so I could see her, get a look at her. If anything, she looked hurt.

"I don't work here that way," she said. "I'm not on the staff."

This encouraged me some but not entirely. "But still you read that stuff, don't you? And you're here."

"I don't see patients. I'm just observing."

I didn't like this last word. Disliked it so much I tried to get up. But she pulled on me and as I said I wasn't feeling so strong.

After I'd fallen back beside her, she said, "I don't think you belong here, okay? I want to help you get out."

I considered this carefully in my mind. But my body was on its own, celebrating already and so soon my mind wasn't really working at all except at trying to control my insides.

"You mean that?"

She smiled and nodded, and I found myself holding on to her when up until now she'd been the only one making gestures.

I liked so much how this felt. She had on a down jacket and I pressed my face into her shoulder and her jacket puffed up around me. I was wearing Gail's jacket, and the rest of my clothes were left-overs. Somebody's jeans, a scrub shirt, a sweater Gail'd brought me when it began to get really cold.

I hadn't seen my things since they took them off me that first day. I hadn't thought about my own things until this minute. It was something about having my face pressed into Beth's coat and knowing it belonged to her. It even smelled like her. This somehow was what started me crying.

I let myself for a while. Let myself for as long as I could because something in me needed to do this and knew it. Still, pretty soon I choked it off. And when I tried to get up this time, instead of pulling me down, Beth got up herself and then helped me.

I fished Gail's pocket for cigarettes. I found her pack pretty fast and pulled one out. A long, skinny Virginia Slim I felt stupid about smoking until I put it in my mouth. It had that nice feel like when you put any cigarette in your mouth after you've kissed somebody, after you've had anything bigger to suck on.

There were matches tucked into the cellophane wrapper. I got them out and lit the cigarette. All this while I half expected Beth to stop me. But she didn't.

I held the pack out to her. She shook her head. Then we started walking, me with one hand holding the cigarette and the other clutching myself around the middle. Beth had her hands clasped behind her back like it was the best way to keep them still. After a while she shoved them into her coat pockets.

I went through that cigarette, and then another. We kept walking but not saying anything more. After the second cigarette she held her hand out and I took it. But soon we were walking with our arms around each other and this purring began working its way through my chest to my stomach and then lower.

I recognized this but pretended I didn't know from where. Kept this up even when we were back in that little room and she was hugging me goodbye. The hugging was making this same feeling all the stronger and bigger and so it took up more space. Ran up into my chest again, and back down. Then was both places at once and everywhere in between. And when she pulled away, it got stronger still, but then seemed to actually follow her until I staggered some from trying to hold on to it.

Ten

The next day Beth took me out walking again. I felt shy for how I'd felt at the end of the day before. Afraid it had showed, while at the same time I wasn't quite admitting it to myself. It seemed important not to let that thing get in the way again. That those feelings would cause the same kind of trouble they had with Ingrid. That if I could just keep from having them, I'd stay safe.

This was the problem—having these feelings, and Beth asking me things. It made me think of Ingrid. The one thing about living the way I'd been living—day-to-day with no thought before or beyond—it'd kept me from thinking about Ingrid and her husband, or about the daughter.

The way I got when Beth asked—and she'd begun asking sooner today, as soon as we sat down against that same log—the way I got let me know that I never stopped thinking about it. That it was always there pulling on me, and me trying not to go under to it.

Today she asked again how it happened. "How did you get here?" she was saying. "I know what it says, but what happened?"

"He had me arrested."

"Who did?" she asked. And I found myself looking at her, and disbelieving, and then slipping away.

"Oh, come on," I said, fighting an urge to get up. Instead I took a pack of cigarettes from Gail's pocket. A fresh one. A pack I had to open. And halfway through doing this I noticed the shape of the pack, noticed my brand.

This little thing stopped me because it didn't seem little at all. And even though Gail had done it, it brought me back closer to Beth.

"I'm sorry," I said. "I thought you'd know. What do you know anyway?"

"Your file says you were arrested for prostitution. That you became violent while resisting arrest. It says you were sent here by an arrangement with the prosecutor's office. The admitting doctor put you in seclusion because of a history of violent behavior."

"Seclusion? Is that what they call it?"

I'd gotten up while she was talking but she stayed put. I paced around a little. Finished the one cigarette and started another.

"That's not how it happened," I said. And I looked closely at her. Tried to see what she believed.

She had the kind of look I remembered from that first time I met her. It'd been the end of the day. Near the end of Gail's shift and so there hadn't been much time. Beth hung on to me. And the look on her face right before she did this was like it had happened to her. Or like she felt what I couldn't feel. Her eyes got so full and her mouth turned soft and then she just pulled me toward her. And though I hadn't remembered it until now, I'd hung on too. I'd buried myself in her like I'd never have to let go, except I did have to.

When she'd pulled away from me, she'd had that same look like the one she had now and I found myself sitting back down beside her, huddled against her, and I said again, "That's not how it happened."

I said this over and over until it became clear I couldn't say what should come next and she let me mumble. She said soothing things in between, said again the thing I'd held on to all night. She said she'd get me out.

A while later she walked me back. Gail met us at the door and told us to hurry because the shift was changing soon and she didn't want to get caught. She meant by the woman coming in next. No one else noticed what went on with me. That was the point, not to notice. The point was for me to be forgotten.

Beth came into the room with me. By the way she lingered I remembered it was Friday. Remembered because I was still counting the days and this was our fifth one together.

We stood there facing each other and over Beth's shoulder I could see Gail in the doorway. I slipped off her coat. She held out her hand for it and then put it on, but still she stood there. She waited for us and I got that shy feeling back and I felt it off Beth too. I knew I did.

Beth stood there an instant longer and she took my hands in hers and then she kissed me. She kissed my cheek. She'd never done this before and I couldn't recover myself. She'd already turned to leave and Gail was talking hurriedly, first to Beth and then me. Talking so fast I lost the first few things she said and after that could only hold on to the cigarette pack she pressed into my hand and the matchbook.

Those two things got me through the weekend. The nurses mostly left me alone, except around feeding time. Even that went smoother because I seemed able to eat.

I picked a corner near the door to spend time in. Usually I took one opposite because being farther away seemed more private, and it let me see what was coming. But this one meant I could smoke and light my own and be pretty sure of not being spotted.

And, crouched there, I thought about Beth. Not about the things I probably should have spent time on, like what to tell her about Ingrid, how much I should say. No, what I thought about was her kissing me and the feel I got off her right before, the shyness. I spent a lot of time wondering what this could mean, or what I wanted it to mean.

I kept it up. I kept it up through the whole weekend. I thought about this moment so much and so long that by the next time I saw her, this one little thing had become so big. Big enough it took up space between us. And as we walked in those woods I felt myself keeping apart from her. Staking actual physical distance. And she seemed to be doing this too. Though I couldn't be sure.

When we got to that log and she sat down, I stayed standing. I stood there for so long saying nothing that finally she said, "Did something happen over the weekend?"

And I wanted to say, "No, just before it." And I started to. But I stopped and only said, "No."

She let this pass. But I could see that if I didn't sit down she'd come back to it. So that's what I did. I sat down with her.

Even so, she said, "Are you sure you're all right? That things are all right?"

I wanted to say no. I wanted so much to tell her every single way things weren't all right, and every way I wasn't. And mostly I wanted to tell her why.

But this time I just said, "Yes." Meaning yes, everything's fine. Because after all, it seemed relative. Fine as last week. Though I knew I dreaded the coming night. Already I knew I wouldn't be able to push it away like before. And I didn't think I could half sleep through it either.

This disability seemed to be about Beth. Not anything she'd said but her having kissed me. It interfered with my capacity to sort things, to keep them cordoned off in my head. That was the other thing about the weekend—things had begun to bleed through. They started seeping into each other until they overlapped in a way that was difficult to control, impossible to put away.

Seeing her again made all this harder and I feared if she touched me some of it would open. That the bleeding and seeping would turn to leaking. That I'd be unable to stop it, and somehow this would give us away. Though I couldn't be sure what this last thing even meant.

Soon after I'd sat down she said, "I've been thinking about you. Thinking what we should do."

She glanced at me after saying this but I kept hidden. I shrugged into Gail's coat, shrunk into it.

"There are steps to getting you out and I think we should start on them. First we've got to get you out of seclusion. As long as you're there, there's no way."

Now I was the one looking at her and looking carefully. She believed what she was saying. I could tell that much. She believed it'd be that simple. Just follow the rules and that's the end of it.

I wanted to stop her right there, say you don't understand, you don't know what's involved, who's involved. I couldn't do it, though. I was afraid if she knew she'd back off. That she'd be safer to me not knowing the risk, not knowing what or who she was up against. That maybe, just maybe, if she didn't know, it might work. She might pull it off.

So this brought me to how much did she have to know, and then to how much could I tell. The curious thing was how much I wanted to tell—to tell her all of it. Same as I wanted to tell her what happened to me every weekday night.

The things stopping me were too hard to make out. Every time I thought I knew what they were and so could face them, they changed form. Then I'd have to regroup, reevaluate. These things kept me mute. And the single thing running underneath, choking off speech, was his belt around my neck.

Beth quit talking. I realized she'd noticed how intently I was watching her. When she quieted, I began thinking things, and below that feeling them, and pretty soon my eyes clouded over. Once my eyes glazed, she put her arm around my shoulders and shook me a little. With that, what I'd worked so hard not to feel began running up and down my thighs—nervous and wanting to stop and stay put somewhere.

"Hey," she said. "What is it?"

I started laughing. Not a real friendly thing to do, but I guess that was the point. I wanted to do the exact opposite—cry—or the thing in between, which seemed this moment to be kissing her. Laughing meant I'd taken the coward's route.

"I'm sorry." I managed to say this much and then managed to take her hand.

"Look," she said. "I'm going to try and get you out of that box. I don't think you can handle it in there too much longer."

This someway bruised me. It seemed a stupid part of me wanted to prove something dumb. To prove I could take it in there the rest of my life if that was needed. To prove I could take anything. At least I kept shut about this. I didn't stand up or bluster. At least I kept myself from doing the half dozen or so things I wanted to do.

We walked back holding hands. Most of the way anyway. As we came into sight of the building she let go and this carried the same shyness or shame that the kiss had. She came into the box with me again. I liked that she'd called it that. That she'd left off using their word for it. A word I didn't like because it made it sound like some fucking retreat or something. Someplace a nun would go.

She didn't stay long, though she had time to. And she stood a little ways back from me instead of right up against me. Her doing this made me realize we didn't exactly know each other. That she'd come out of nowhere for me and me for her. That we'd gotten in deep with each other, and fast. That we'd gotten there out of nothing but feeling and need. I had with her, anyway.

I had no way to know anything about her. But still it seemed I did know. Knew that underneath all her command she carried something I'd hooked and was sorry for. Though I wasn't above using it. I was that desperate for help.

Of course, seeing it this way was easier than seeing how it was. That was all about what she'd hooked in me and kept pulling at. Whatever that was seemed too messy to name. Like if I let it spread out from my chest, it'd take over my body. It'd maybe get to my mind.

It was already hard enough to cope in here. I couldn't contend with something like that. And so instead of letting it up, I pushed it down. I put it into my belly and then lower until it could be all about pressing against her. All about her body. The things I wanted to do to it and do to her, and with her, and have her do to me. But not here. And so we stayed standing in this way that caused problems—a little apart with her holding my hands and her eyes holding mine, and me trying to keep pace until I had to look away.

Gail saved me. She came to get her coat and I let go of Beth. And then she left. She slipped away while Gail and I talked. She did this without a word, and so left me wondering if she'd ever come back or was she finished? Had she seen some of the same stuff that I had and wanted to get away from it? Or had I maybe just been someway too mean?

Eleven

Beth must've pulled somebody's string besides mine because by the end of the week they'd moved me. It was still lockup but that beat the lockbox and so I couldn't quite complain. This didn't mean I had company, though. The others on the floor were the lifers. Women so old they'd had actual surgery. Others, a little bit younger, had the chemical kind, daily.

This meant you heard the same things over and over. Watched the same shuffling. Except for one woman, a little one, who moved fast and hit her palm with her fist over and over, saying, "Whip, whip. Cut, cut."

This was stuff you could no way ask about, but Gail told me some of it. The ones who'd been cut had had it done early—thirteen, twelve. They'd been here ever since. Likewise the ones in their fifties and sixties—once their trouble started they'd never been given the chance to escape it.

So this wasn't a place where people got better. This was a holding pattern and these women holdovers. Given my patron, none of this should've surprised me. But still it did—the kind of place in old movies. The kind that didn't exist anymore and so how could any of us? The perfect place to lose someone forever.

So this explained what I was doing here. And maybe it explained Beth's wanting so bad to get me out. These next few weeks she spent coaching me for this. A big moment before some committee of doctors. I hadn't seen a doctor since I'd landed here so it surprised me to hear them mentioned. Surprised me anyone actually ran this place.

When the day came, I sat at the foot of a long wooden table and went through the motions. Ten or twelve men I'd never seen in my life asked me ten or twelve different questions. And afterward, since I'd had no expectations myself, I worried about Beth. About how hard she might've hoped. And, too, I worried what might happen now that they'd noticed me.

Beth had stayed behind with them, so Gail took me back. She sat with me on my bed—at least I had an actual one of those now.

When Beth came in, she was all red faced and shaky. She kept saying she didn't understand. That she couldn't see why they'd said no. How the reasons they gave didn't make sense.

I looked to Gail but she'd already gotten most of the way out the door, so I looked back at Beth. She paced the small room. Kept walking back and forth from the now-closed door to the window. It was open with a cold breeze coming through the metal grate.

I let her stammer and walk. Worked hard at ignoring this pull to get up, to put my arms around her. Ignored wanting to stop her. Soon enough she stopped herself. She hadn't actually looked at me so far and now when she did I looked away, then realized in an instant how that would look to her.

She came and sat down beside me, and I felt her hand on the back of my neck, her fingers in my hair. I felt her trying to soothe me and then she said, "I'm so sorry," and still I didn't tell her. Didn't say a word about Ingrid or Ingrid's husband.

The next day she and I went back to the woods. We sat in the leaves, propped against that log there and I listened while she said, "I don't understand it," and "It doesn't make sense." I listened while she said these things over and over, and only once did she look at me in a way that required an answer.

What could I say to her? I kept my head down and of course she took that as disappointment. She pulled me closer to her and I held on to her and she apologized over and over until I was nearly crying. Not for me, but for her. I couldn't risk it, though. I couldn't risk telling her because that seemed to equal losing her, though this way I seemed to be losing her anyway.

Two more weeks like this and then everything changed. She and I came back from one of our walkabouts. Came back to find Gail standing at the door and waving. And as we got closer, she said, "Come on. Come on, hurry," which confused me because it seemed to me we were on the early side.

Beth said, "What is it?"

"I've got to take her over. She's got a visitor."

I started backing up. Beth felt this, I think, because she tightened her hand on my arm and this steadied me a little.

I don't know what my face looked like but Beth took one look and said to Gail, "Let me take her. You're about to go home. You don't want to get held up here."

Then Gail was looking at me too. Seemed not sure what to do or to say. I tried to smile at her but I felt sick and so I wasn't sure how it came off. I was caught. I figured it'd be Ingrid's husband, and so I wanted Gail bringing me. But in the time it took to think this much Beth and I were already walking over to the main building.

We stopped at the desk and the woman there pointed us to a room at the end of the hall. The door was ajar, but you couldn't see in. By now I'd gone on automatic. I'd flicked some switch some-where inside me that would let me get through this, would get me through anything, and so I thought I was prepared and I guess I was, except not for Ingrid.

As we pushed open the door I saw her standing by the window, one that didn't have a grate on it. She turned toward me and I felt like I ran to her but instead I was standing stock still with Beth nudging me. Beth closed the door behind us and stood leaning back against it. She'd let go after pushing me. Ingrid had made some progress partway to me but then she'd stopped. It was up to me to close the distance remaining.

I found my feet and began walking. And when I got close enough I held out my hand and she pulled me against her. Then she was kissing me and I was kissing her back, all the time feeling Beth behind me, watching.

Still, I couldn't stop this. My coat was open and Ingrid had her hands underneath it and then under my shirt. I had my hands on her, too, but just holding on, trying to keep my balance while really I was falling into her.

She had her hand on my stomach. Had my pants already partway open. This made me glad for the bulk of my coat, which was no longer Gail's but one Beth had brought me. By now I had both my hands cradling Ingrid's neck. I couldn't get my tongue far enough into her mouth. I couldn't help myself and then she'd gotten her hand into my underwear and my knees went loose and I opened my legs and sank against her. Felt her hand inside me and then I heard the door slam.

I don't know if that alone straightened me up. Or if it was knowing that with Beth gone, someone else would be in here and fast. I staggered away, buttoning my coat because my pants seemed too intricate to manage and then someone else was already there. I recognized the guard, and him me. He smirked, looked us both up and down and then plopped into a chair.

This didn't leave much for me and Ingrid to do except talk. But soon enough it became clear that this had been the point all along. That what had come before was merely the warm-up to some kind of favor.

"He found me," she said.

And, now, since we weren't touching, I had my bearings. "No kidding," I said. "Me, too."

I saw her expression change but then change back again. "I'm going back to him," she said. "I already have. He doesn't know I came here. He doesn't know I know where you are. I had to tell him things. I had to say you put me up to leaving. You did in a way. You know this."

She looked at me when she said it. I looked at my guard. He was licking the corner of his mouth. Then he ran his finger there, along his moustache and down his chin, through the rest of his beard. I found myself rubbing my cheek and then quickly looking away from him and back to her and then down at the floor.

"Look, I think he'll let up on you. I think so. Now I'm back I think maybe he'll forget about you."

Now I was the one wanting to storm out slamming the door. Instead I sat down on a couch. One that faced the chair this guard was sitting in. And it was good that I did because my head had fogged and my feet hurt and I felt suddenly very tired.

I wasn't sure what she was asking of me. I wasn't at all sure why she'd come and, without quite realizing it, I asked her. I said, "Ingrid, why are you here?"

"I didn't want you to think I deserted you."

I began laughing. I couldn't help it.

She became flustered. She said, "Really I haven't known very long. I only got back three months ago."

Her saying this snapped me back. I'd no idea how long I'd been here but I suppose I'd been telling myself it'd only been a few weeks. Hearing otherwise fucked with me deeply. My face began to tremble. I could feel it and I guess she could see it because she said, "I've got to leave. I've stayed too long already."

She came over to me on her way to the door. My hand was resting on my knee and she put hers over it. I felt it brush across and then she hurried to the door.

My guard let me sit there until we'd both heard the end of her footsteps. Then he gave a long low whistle and got up. He pulled me by the arm and took me back. And later that night he was the one visiting me.

Twelve

I figured that'd be the last I'd see of Beth. I figured I might even land back in the lockbox. Instead she came the next day as if nothing had happened. Or, almost. We walked out to our same place in the woods but without talking or touching and this let me know she wasn't going to pretend it away.

Even once we sat down, though, she waited a while. Waited as if she expected me to just start telling her. I suppose this would've been the normal thing to do. And I suppose I had no reason left not to, had nothing to lose now.

Still, out of habit, I made her ask and what she asked first was, "Who is she?"

I didn't know how to explain easily and so I had trouble starting—didn't know quite where to start until it seemed best to be blunt.

"Her husband was a regular for a while. He took me home to her and I stayed a few days. And then a few weeks. It became very complicated."

I'd been staring at the leaves and now I picked one up and pulled it apart.

Beth didn't say anything and so I figured I hadn't said enough. But while I was trying to come up with more but stay along the same lines she said, "Are you in love with her?"

This took me aback. Both because she asked and because I'd never thought about it in this way. I felt like saying, "not after yesterday," but that seemed flip and hurtful—not the best thing to say.

Not saying it left me dumb and this probably left her assuming my answer and not the one I expected she wanted to hear. The answer she wanted? I feared I'd just now happened on to it. Had only just realized, or even considered it. And it seemed it would've been okay to tell her, tell her what she wanted to hear, if only she hadn't needed to hear it.

So I worked on deciding she didn't want me to say it. Did this so I'd be able to. But somehow, once I'd convinced myself I was wrong after all, that she didn't want me to tell her I loved her instead of Ingrid. Once I'd accomplished this, it made the telling even less likely instead of possible.

All this left my head swimming. It made me want to get up and walk around. As if higher altitude would clear things a little. As if getting a little farther away from Beth would. But getting up wasn't possible. The physical motion involved wasn't. And so instead I sat there looking at my hands, at the spine of another leaf I'd dismantled.

Beth didn't ask me again and after a while it could be like she'd never asked in the first place, but not quite. She put her arm around me and for a moment I thought she was going to kiss me except both of us at the last minute seemed to move away from this and not toward it.

I lit a cigarette and this changed things again. Got her back to talking. Asking more questions but along a different track and so everything eased some.

"How long did you stay with them?" This was her first question.

"I don't know," I said. "A month, maybe two. Or maybe it was only weeks, I'm not sure."

She looked like she didn't understand how I couldn't know. She looked like that was what she would ask more about but instead she asked, "Why, why did you stay?"

"Money," I said, though if Ingrid saw the lie in this Beth no doubt would too. I told myself she hadn't seen me with them, only with Ingrid. Told myself maybe this made a difference. Whether it did or not, Beth let this one by.

"What did you do?" she said next.

This pissed me off, so I said, "What do you think I did? I fucked them and they fucked me. Pretty thoroughly."

I could practically feel her trying to be patient, trying to hold her temper.

"No, I mean …" But she stopped here as if that had been what she meant after all. That she'd needed to know for sure, hear me say it.

She got up, which was not something she'd done before, and it left me sitting there alone so I lit another cigarette. She ran her fingers through her hair. Pushed it out of her eyes, though it hadn't been there to begin with, and I found myself looking at her differently.

Or maybe I was just noticing how I always looked at her. Then I was getting up too and we were walking back, though it was still quite early.

Since I'd gotten moved out of the hole and into this room, Beth didn't usually linger. We had more of an audience here. Today, though, when she started to leave, I stopped her. Had a surge of bad feeling and wanted to help her.

"He's the one put me in here," I said.

"What do you mean?"

"He had me picked up. Made sure they put me here. Her husband."

She looked uncomprehending. Like this didn't make sense at all and so I felt stupid for telling her. Figured now she'd think I was paranoid or something. Once they get you in a place like this people don't believe you so easy. But then I guess that's a big part of the point—making sure you're walking uphill with each thing you say.

I could see this as good news though. My lack of credibility might make the things Ingrid said possible. Maybe her husband would move on. Maybe he only needed to be able to say I'd been here, not keep me here forever.

As I passed this idea back and forth, Beth just stood there. Stood there with this dull look on her face and I couldn't tell what, if anything, was going on behind it.

She'd taken my arm but I hadn't really realized it. I'd been too lost in my own head and only felt her now because she wobbled a little. I found myself taking her hand to steady her, leading her over to sit on the bed, but once we were there she recovered herself and said, "No, wait. You've reminded me of something. I've got to go and take care of something."

I watched her go, wondering what she could possibly mean. What it might mean for me. Whether I should worry or hope. All of this pummeled me—the things I'd told her and wished I hadn't. But mostly it was that deadened urgency she'd had as she hurried away, rushing in some stumbling trance. And me? I was left there picking myself up. Left to consider more immediate things like would I be let alone tonight? And left knowing the chances against it since I was still the freshest thing going.

The next day Beth started jittery and kept that way. She hurried us out. Seemed all the while to be looking over her shoulder. Even once we were in the woods she still spoke in whispers. "My husband is in the DA's office. I'm going to get you out."

"You are or he is?"

I asked this meanly, my own sharpness surprising me and the cause of it tweaking me worse.

I knew she was married. Knew it all along. She wore a ring for Chrissakes. But somehow so long as she didn't mention him I didn't care. It was like he didn't exist or didn't matter. But her saying this had me picturing someone she went home to. Someone I might soon be beholden to. No, I didn't think so. I didn't think that'd work real well.

"He's going to try and find out what happened."

"I told you what happened. You think your husband can go against this guy? He bought your husband's boss years ago and now somehow ... Tell me, by magic?"

I'd hurt her. That was clear. I only now realized I hadn't wanted to.

She looked at her hands when she spoke next. She said, "I don't know. He said he'd look into it. See what he could do."

I found myself digging dirt with my heel. Making a trench through the leaves. I chewed my tongue to keep from crying because it'd come to me that my upset wasn't really about her husband. It was about the chance she was offering. I realized it when I thought about the night before. That same bitch sitting by the door, and that same guy on top of me, and me trying to decide was he fucking me senseless or had I been there all along?

I believed if I stayed here much longer I'd go senseless forever. Walk around speechless or with one or two favorite phrases. Wind up in that state without the aid of anyone cutting my brain or pumping anything into it. I had those constant reminders pacing the floor. All day I'd watch them because what else was there to look at?

Beth had come to be all of that—the what else. I struggled with myself, finally got so far as, "Do you think …?"

"Yes," was what she said. And then we didn't talk so much but just sat there and I found myself wanting all kinds of things from her. Things I couldn't quite put words to. Or wouldn't put words to because it all seemed too blunt for that and maybe too big. I leaned against her and she held my hand in both of hers. And this seemed like something I could count on, if that had ever been something I'd known how to do.

Thirteen

She did get me out and it didn't even take very long. The way she explained it, her husband worked it underground, slid it by. No big fuss, which was the smart way to play it, except it left me wondering what would happen if Ingrid's husband found out. Wondering how he hadn't already. Though this I could chalk up to his moving on. To my never holding anyone's notice for very long.

I worked at not worrying. And then at not thinking about it at all, and soon enough I stopped. I had other things occupying me— this new stupid job very much like the old stupid one and trying hard not to do anything afterward, trying just to go home.

Going home was easier because I had my own place now. A small apartment Beth had helped me find. My view was a pharmacy and I liked watching the neon sign flashing DRUGS in fancy pink script all night long. It kept me company.

Beth did too. Part of the deal with my getting out was I'd see her. They'd made her part of the package. Stamped her right on my ticket. So here I was with this new life, which wasn't different enough from the old one.

Anyway, her office wasn't far from where I was living. Close enough you could walk it, though I had my car back. Beth's husband had had his hand in this too. Apparently the thing had sat in that parking lot piling tickets until finally they'd towed it. I sure didn't have the money to bail it, so they wangled it, which way I never did get clear. I understood clearly about the favors, though. And, being me, already I worried about payback time. I wasn't keen on owing so much to a couple. I mean, look where I ended up when the couple owed me.

I kept pushing these things to the back of my brain. If I'd let myself think too much about any of them, or all of them, I wouldn't have made it to work in the mornings. And I sure wouldn't have made it to Beth's office afterward.

That's how it had begun to line up—most every day now I saw her. Though how or when it had turned to that often, I'd been unaware. It seemed almost like something someone else had decided and not her. Except it was her.

Sometimes I got there as the other people were leaving—the people she worked with, the shrinks and all. Usually I'd wait this little time out in my car because I hated how they looked at me. The way their friendliness gave away everything going on underneath it. Sometimes I sat there so long she'd have to come get me. And when she did, I liked how she put her arm around me while we walked in together.

But once we were in her office, it always took me a while to sit down. I'd kind of wander around, though it wasn't a big enough room to keep that going for long. She'd ask me how work had been and we'd start out talking small like that for a bit. Then finally I'd sit down when I thought she might not notice I hadn't been sitting all along.

I sat in this chair opposite her. She didn't have a couch. This was probably a good thing because, after all, if you're having trouble sitting, how much more trouble are you going to have lying down?

I'd behaved this way from the very first day. Not the sitting in my car part, but the rest of it. Now that I was out I didn't know how to be with her. I felt embarrassed about the way it had been between us. The way we'd been before. And I thought maybe she did too because we were both like that—shy of each other and cautious. Neither one knowing where to start and, for me, this was made worse by feeling there was nothing to say. So I stumbled around to keep from talking.

I guess that's how the small talk had begun. That very first day with her asking about my first day at work, and those first days always the same. Going by in a blur and leaving you shaky and faltering. Making you feel like maybe you should go back to the thing you're good at. Making me feel that way. That pull already there and somehow surprising me.

If she knew this too she didn't say so. But once I'd got myself sitting down and we'd finished with the weather and the rest of that kind of thing she said, "So how did it start for you?"

If it hadn't taken me so long to get into that chair I would've gotten back up because this is what they all ask. The ones buying it. Sooner or later they do. If you're young anyway. And while she phrased it different, I wasn't sure she meant it any different so I teased her along. I said, "How did what start?"

I said this mostly because I wanted to hear how she'd put it. What she'd call it. But she didn't say anything, which was probably smart.

Her not talking meant neither of us said anything for a while. And just when I thought I wouldn't be talking to her ever again I began telling her. And I began hating her some because I knew I wanted to tell her. I don't mean I wanted to tell someone and she happened to be there and asking. What I mean is I wanted her to be the one I told it all to.

But I didn't think she wanted to be listening. I could see in her eyes how she felt. And it wasn't what I expected. Not that I could have said what that had been, just that I didn't think it'd be standard. She looked like she might cry or like she was angry. She looked a lot like she had the day Ingrid came to see me.

I stood up to go because this seemed over. But when I started for the door, she got up quickly and held on to me. It was the same thing we'd done all along. But this time it felt different. Being here felt different. I let her hang on for a while. And I held her, too, because, near as I could tell, it seemed to be what she needed. And because doing this reminded me we weren't new to each other.

She sort of pressed into me and nothing was terribly plain about it—the same way I couldn't pin down what I did to her, or could let it go by if I wanted. I could tell you I put my hands on her ass only because it made it easier to keep my balance. I could almost offer this explanation and believe it myself while still knowing the other. But then having two things going on at the same time is not something I question. It's just something I do. Something we all do. Everyone does. All the time.

Beth wasn't much shorter than me but I always felt huge around her. My hands large and marauding and her small underneath them. I didn't pay so much attention to her hands. Not at first I didn't. But then she put one on my back pretty low. The other one, she kept moving it around on my neck. Not her whole hand, just the heel of her palm. And then she'd tucked her fingers inside my collar, stroking soft there until my knees started to bend.

I don't know which of us broke away first. I remember her asking me to come back and sit down, and I did this. Sat there all gangly and loose and trying to make sense of the questions she asked. Being slow about this, what with not having any blood in my brain.

She seemed okay, just nervous a little. She said, "What made you try to run out?"

I had to stall because I didn't remember. Not right off, so I said, "What, was I running?"

"You seemed in a hurry."

There was this little catch in her voice that would give me a way in if I took it. But at the same time it reminded me of what made me get up and so I left her alone. I couldn't see telling her it'd been the way she acted, how she'd gone all hot in the face.

I stonewalled her. I said, "I don't know. I guess I felt tired of telling you things."

She seemed not at all satisfied with this but she let it go. "Do you still want to leave?"

I didn't, of course, but that was all about wanting her touching my neck and not at all about talking. I supposed if talking would lead us back there, I'd do it. I said, "No, I don't want to leave. Not anymore. It's okay now."

I'd forgotten what I'd been saying to her. It sure hadn't taken long to tell her my first time, blowing that guy for the twenty. I remembered that much. Where we'd gotten to after that? I didn't know.

She said it was Ingrid's husband, my first time with him. She said I'd told her how he hadn't seemed to come from the train but from somewhere behind me, that then I'd gotten up.

Now I told her he'd asked me was I looking for something. And that it had caught me off guard because that's the kind of thing we usually say to them. Right there he'd flipped the game, right from the start.

"And you felt?"

"Interested," I said, which was true, but I left out wary and guarded. And I left out afraid because it wasn't the image I had of myself, especially not of myself working. It sure wasn't something I ever wanted a client to see and I didn't want her seeing me this way either. Already I found myself measuring her all the time, trying to find where she fit.

"Why interested?" she asked.

"Because he didn't act like the others. He didn't check his watch or look around. He didn't act like he'd ever be explaining anything to anyone waiting at home."

She didn't say anything to this and so I went back to what happened, told her how he'd come right out with what he'd wanted. She asked me what that was and I had some trouble telling her. I had to keep myself from getting up again. Settled for shifting my legs around.

"What did he want?" she asked again and her voice was so soft I could almost say I hadn't heard her but instead I said, "He wanted to fuck my ass."

I didn't look at her when I said it and she wasn't looking at me. I knew this because when I did look at her she was lost out the window. And I could tell that was where she'd been for a while.

"You agreed?" she said, still looking out there and so now I could look at her.

"Uh-huh," I said, but I didn't say anything more.

She said, "What happened?"

It was her voice, how gentle it was; this let me tell her. I said, "We got into his car—in the front seat. He told me to take off my underwear.

"I did what he said. Then I started to reach for him but he took my wrist. He said, 'I don't want you to do that.'

"He told me to lift up my skirt. He looked for a while, then he touched me and I sort of … See, I don't usually, but they don't usually. It was the way I started breathing and he knew, he said, 'Come on.'

"He pulled me out after him; pushed me onto my stomach on the backseat. I was half on my knees and half lying down and it started out not so easy because I couldn't give in."

I stopped here because telling her was putting me back there and I needed something from her. She seemed maybe to know this because she met my eyes and the look in hers—I felt like I'd never been cared for this way.

I began talking again. But now my voice was broken and soft and not behaving. "It hurt," was what I said. "It hurt a lot. That way it does at first if you can't ease up. But then he said, 'Come on, kiddo, we had a deal.'

"He put his hand under my belly and then lower and it got easier. Up until the end it did."

I stopped again. I wanted Beth. She was still gazing at me that same way, and at first I liked it. At first I handled it, but then I had to look down.

When I did this she asked, "What happened at the end?" She had that same catch in her voice, only this time, what with where I was, it made me wary, tempted me to play her. I looked at her for a little while.

"What happened at the end?" she said again. "What made it hard for you?"

And something about her, or me, or what I needed to say, made me shift, made me hard, but I still told her.

"He got me to come, okay? That was his thing. He'd get me to come and, I don't know, always before he did. And then I'd be in that place of not feeling so good and he'd …"

"What happened that time?"

"He got me turned over. He got me turned over on my back. And he put his knee up between my legs and he got me to suck him.

But he still didn't come. And I hadn't said I'd blow him and then he jerked himself off anyway. All in my face, in my hair, like before, like he always ..."

"Like when?"

"That night with Ingrid." And now I didn't know how I'd gotten here from there, from where I'd been talking. I looked at Beth. I looked to her for help with the how of this. But seeing her convinced me I'd made some mistake. She'd stiffened to where I thought she'd get up but she didn't and I didn't either, though I felt this pull to, not to leave but to go to her.

We stayed dead here, neither of us saying anything more. It left me lodged between shame and anger—left me wanting something to hold that could hurt me.

She spoke first. She said, "What exactly went on with you and Ingrid?"

"I don't know," I said, and it was true. It'd been something I couldn't explain to myself because I could never explain Ingrid or my importance to her. I couldn't believe my importance to her, and it did keep changing. One day with her wanting me and another day not. One day her playing his wife in on the game and another pretending her ignorance of it.

And me, well it left me not a bit easier to see myself in this. And instead of lending compassion or understanding I found hatred. Stronger for her than for him. Him, I could dismiss. Or at least pretend to.

These were all things I thought but didn't give voice to. I could hardly keep them sorted in my head. I feared terribly what might happen if I let them come out of my mouth. A sleepiness always attended this kind of thinking. An inability to press on with it, and instead a tremendous pull to give in, to give up. And to get up I suppose, too, because that's in fact what I did, almost without realizing it.

It wasn't the hurried run to the door like before but more a walking slumber and maybe for this reason Beth didn't follow. I was in the waiting room, almost to the door, before she caught up with me. We sat down on a couch there and I sank so easily into her. I rested. And I didn't feel her arms or her hands but just felt her as one complete thing to lean on.

I don't know how long the two of us stayed that way. Don't know whether I actually slept or if I stayed in this place so nearby it. I do recall waking up, or something similar to that. She'd shifted her body and I started. Jumped up, only to find myself on my knees on the floor. I couldn't have said what was happening. I remember claiming my leg had fallen asleep, "with the rest of me," I think I said, trying to laugh about it.

She watched me from the couch, seeming dazed herself and uncomprehending. It was as if the emotions had been sucked from each of us and she looked pale from it. I didn't know whether I should leave, just leave her there.

I got back on my feet. Tested myself by walking around. I didn't know the time and there wasn't a clock in easy view. I considered picking up the phone. Finding out that way because suddenly it seemed a very important thing to know. And while Beth wore a watch, I realized I wouldn't believe what it said.

I let all this pass before I sat down with her. She'd regained herself. She said, "I think you better leave." I didn't question her. I simply did what she said.

On my way home, I drove past the train station. This wasn't planned or unusual, it was simply the easiest way home, or the second easiest. The route I took most often and usually without too much notice. It was too late for commuters and, while I wanted to, I didn't drive through the lot. And I didn't think about wanting to. I didn't dwell on it. Instead I saw it as something natural. Something bound to happen at one time or another.

Fourteen

I went to bed easily that night, what with being already asleep before I got there. Waking up, then, was the hard part. I guess Beth and I had had a late night if I thought back to it. I didn't get home until sometime like midnight and here I was getting up again. All those hours asleep on her couch making me somehow less rested instead of more.

I went through the motions at work. And they seemed untroubled by this version, which was friendly if a little hazy. They didn't know me any differently. By midafternoon I caught myself already watching the clock, already fidgety.

I took my afternoon break at the bar across the street. Just a quick shot to even me out from all the coffee I'd needed just to wake myself up. I was sure that must be the cause of my anxiousness. After work I stopped by the bar again. I had two drinks this time. And I didn't stay for more because if I did I'd be late to her office.

I got there as I did yesterday, when everyone else was leaving. Sat pretending to read magazines and trying not to catch anyone's eye. Trying especially not to catch her eye because she was standing there, too. Was saying goodbye to people. And I watched her the same way she seemed to be watching me—around the corners of things.

After they'd all cleared out, we went into her office, with her following me and closing the door. I did my walkabout thing while she sat down and began asking me stuff, same as yesterday, same as yesterday's small talk.

I could feel her eyeing me and I kept from looking back at her. I did this for as long as I could because it seemed if I met her eyes I'd be embarrassed for standing and then I'd sit down before I was ready to. So I put my eyes to the things on her shelves, the books and small objects. Ran my fingers along some of them but didn't really touch anything.

I did all this so intently it took me time to see she wasn't saying much anymore, not asking me stuff. The silence made everything heavy, especially my limbs. I headed for the chair, following my legs as if they remembered the way by themselves and I was just watching.

Once I sat down she kept quiet for a time, finally saying, "You look tired."

I didn't say anything back, not right off. Instead I looked at her for the first time that day. She didn't look tired and I wondered why not. I wondered why she should've gotten any more rest than I did. I had to work to keep from turning this into something between us, something annoying to me.

"I'm okay," I finally said.

"Your job's all right?"

Here I sharpened because I remembered she'd asked about this already. "I just said so, didn't I?" I didn't say this meanly, just flat, nearly a question.

She said, "I didn't know if you meant it."

I looked away, trying to understand what about her was making me so mad. And I was trying to hide this anger while I tried to fathom it. I sank farther into the chair. My legs ached terribly. Even my hands hurt, and I tried to explain this as the demands of my job. That I wasn't used to being on my feet all day. I tried to believe this but didn't even come close.

This didn't feel like that kind of tired—not something coming from within. This felt imposed from outside and pressing down, and so it made me want to struggle against it. But all the time I knew I'd lose. And I wanted to lose. Because though I was trying to tell myself it wasn't true, the pull had something very sweet to it, something pretending safety.

I looked up at her, though this took some effort because my head had grown as burdensome as the rest of me. I had to shift myself down, let the back of the chair support it.

She said, "Do you want to tell me some more about Ingrid?"

I looked at her wondering if I had missed something, because feeling the way I did I might have. "Were we talking about her?" I asked.

"Yesterday," Beth said.

I remembered nothing so I didn't know where to begin. I got hung up because I didn't want her to know I'd lost this ground. And I didn't know how to cover myself. I sat there marooned and she kept at me.

"What was she to you?"

"Nothing," I said in a way that made the opposite obvious. Still I kept on this line and said, "A client. She got him to buy me, okay? Is that what you want to know? How it worked?"

"I want to know what she meant."

"I told you. Nothing."

"That's not how it looked the day she came to see you."

"Oh, and how did that look?" I felt clearer getting hot at her, not so sleepy. For this reason I wanted to keep it going, to needle her some, so I said, "What was it made you run out?"

"I didn't like watching it."

She said this very quietly. And I saw her say it, though she wasn't looking at me anymore.

I hadn't expected her to admit even this much. Off base in this way, I felt myself loosening. And so when she held her hand out to me, I took it. Then we were standing and had our arms around each other. I wanted badly to kiss her. And this wanting and not being able seemed so familiar.

She'd tucked her head beneath mine and I could feel her cheek along my neck and her mouth on my shoulder, her hand pulling my collar away. Her dress was the kind that showed a lot of her shoulders and some of her back and I slid my hand underneath it. Believed this could seem accidental.

What she did was lean into me very lax and so I held her tighter. I felt myself going that same way—taut and slack all at once. This made it very hard to stay on my feet. With both of us so heavy there was this tremendous drag toward the floor. I wanted at least to be on my knees.

I staggered away from her and back into my chair. The door seemed where I should go, but just too far away. She stayed standing a while longer. She looked like she was trying hard to remember something, but then her face colored and she sat down. I found myself wondering about the night before. Wondering until it grew flimsier instead of more solid. And then I wondered how much anyone can know of the things they desire too much, these being the most frightening of all and sometimes with good reason.

This thinking led me easily back to Ingrid. And out of something I didn't recognize in myself, but still knew to be mine, I said,

"I thought I loved her. She'd say these things to me. I knew better than that. I shouldn't've ..."

"What did she say?"

Beth's voice coming the way it did, completely flat and protected and trailing off—it was enough to stop me from where I was going. Kept me from being stupid a second time. At least for now. I stopped talking and started fidgeting, not in any evident way but inside myself.

To look at her, she'd done the opposite. Gone so lost and still she seemed not even to notice the quiet. What we did for a long time was just sit there. She'd fixed on some point out the window. And I'd fixed on her. Not restless now, but caught in the same place she was. This brought me to a point of wanting to offer her something. But I was unable to think what that should be.

Like last night, what she finally asked of me was to leave. I felt stung by this, by her. I got up wanting to lash back but swallowed it. And when I did, I found my throat already crowded with other things. I comforted myself with a plan of how to get back. Not at her, but at myself.

And so that's how I left—knowing exactly what I'd do, just not knowing when.

Fifteen

The next day Beth called me at work. She told me she wanted me to show up fifteen minutes later. I said, sure, that it'd be fine, thinking how this would give me time for an extra drink after work.

She stayed on the line like she had more to say. I had customers waiting, so I said, "Was there something else?"

She said no, she guessed not. Then we hung up, and I went back to work with my hands shaking a little, and the rest of me limp and asleep and expectant.

When I got to her place that evening, no one was there. No one but her and I was glad. I even imagined she'd realized my discomfort and had done this rescheduling for me. I'd had four drinks in rapid succession, standing at the bar—the corner of it by the door. And now, in her office, I found it easier to sit down. I still couldn't manage it right off the way I suspected you were supposed to, but at least I didn't drag it out too long.

Already she seemed quieter than usual and when I sat down I noticed this more. I realized she hadn't yet said a word or asked me a question and I looked up quickly to see if she was there at all. I was suddenly scared she'd gone lost already. Done this even before me. But the look on her face was so sharp it seemed nearly grim and I felt myself smiling.

She didn't amuse me. This smile was more of the same kind of fear, just angled different. I began chewing my tongue to try and change the look on my face. "What is it?" I said when this didn't work either. But I guess she didn't know how she seemed because she said, "Nothing," and it sounded convincing.

She didn't ask me anything about work and I didn't volunteer anything. I worried maybe I looked drunk or acted it. I didn't think this possible after only four drinks—well, and those two in the afternoon. If anything, though, I felt like I could've used one more. Especially since once she began asking me stuff she went right back to Ingrid.

I didn't mean to, but I became uncooperative. I could've talked to her about the rest of it but not this part. I felt stupid about what I'd said the day before. That I'd let on as much as I had. And then she'd gone and left me by myself with it. Had gone off somewhere, where it bothered her, too, but in another way. Some way I needed to understand but couldn't yet.

I didn't know the place safely between us and so what else could I do but stop altogether or at least try to? I hated her vacant but this sharpness was even worse. Its edges cut up all the space between us. Left it stirred around and cloudy. I would've gotten back on my feet but I knew what would happen when I did that and I wanted to save it.

"Is she why you stayed?"

"I don't know," I said. "Not exactly. It's hard to know where he stopped and she started. What was what. I don't remember it well."

This was the sort of stuff I said to her. And the last thing most of all seemed a con, though true at that moment. The rest of the time I remembered what had happened with them, with Ingrid and him. The rest of the time I couldn't get rid of it. But sitting here with Beth reordered everything and then moved it some more until it didn't make any sense and was hard to recall.

That's when the way out, the way back, seemed so necessary and all about Beth. About touching her. But then each and every time, she'd wind up where I'd been—lost and dazed—and then what brought me back was getting hot. Angry, I mean, but the other way too. That other way running underneath and governing everything between us. There all the time, but never acknowledged.

For now at least I could still talk and she could too. She said, "What do you remember?"

"Little things that don't mean anything." But this wasn't true either, so when she asked what things these were, I found myself telling her other things, found myself saying, "She said we'd run off together. I didn't want to because I didn't believe her. I didn't believe she would or that we could.

"I saw myself as just the push anyway. I didn't want to be around her when she realized this. We'd only wind up fighting."

I didn't plan to go on, but Beth said, "Tell me what you mean."

"If we left, she'd find out I wasn't who she wanted. Who she'd made me into. I mean, how long do you think it'd take?"

Beth didn't say anything to this and I found I kept talking maybe just to fill the space.

"I didn't want to end up there so I didn't believe we were going at all. That she'd ever be able to. I didn't believe it until I woke up alone in that house.

"But I didn't have to think about it much. I had to get out fast. I had to get out before he came back. I didn't think about whether I should've done something different. Not until I wound up in that car with those cops, anyway. Until I saw how long his reach was, and that he would bother with me, in a way she never would."

I stopped here because this last thing put me in a place I didn't know. I hadn't thought this way before and so I wanted to grasp it. But stop it, too. Stop it before I said anything else like it.

I glanced at Beth because I hadn't been keeping an eye on her and had just now noticed it. She was looking right at me. This put me further off base because until then I thought maybe she hadn't been paying attention. Realizing she was confused me all the more because I'd been both wanting her to and not. Or I'd been wanting her to but at the same time was afraid of it.

I knew how I would've felt if she'd gone blank, but I couldn't make out what this other thing felt like. I only knew it made me want to go somewhere else. And that's what I did because I wound up standing, though I didn't go anywhere far. I didn't even go to the door, but instead to the window and then I knew I was waiting for her.

When she came up behind me I first felt a kind of relief. But then a trembling because it was different to have her behind me and with her arms around my waist. Different enough I turned around to face her so I'd feel less bare, more in command. Or at least I thought I would except I couldn't find any kind of force anywhere in my being. Instead I fell against her body in a way that would've allowed anything.

She seemed to go toward this. I felt her hands under my shirt, on my back for a moment, before she put them to a more familiar place on my neck. I was so slack, I felt all this very intently. Felt it so much there was nothing else for a while. And maybe not for her either because her breathing turned from shallow to deep and I could feel her against my chest and then felt her lower, pressing against me until it was my turn to hold her up.

We didn't stop this time but we didn't go further. It stayed the way it was—both obvious and impossible. The kind of thing I could easily keep from putting words to, could keep in someplace I'd think about later or never. This time, though, I wondered how she did it. How she thought about it and where in her mind she kept it.

I got home. Or at least I'd gotten my car parked and was sitting in it. I did this for a space of time I couldn't measure, but then started the engine again and began driving around. I ached from having nowhere to go. I don't mean heartache but a soreness in my muscles—a tiredness that was becoming familiar to me and so, maybe to stop it, I drove past her office.

I saw her car still there but no light on. Both wondered and knew what she might be doing, but the work of maintaining these two strands at once just tired me more.

Sixteen

That I found myself at the train station that night would probably surprise no one. But it did surprise me. Afterward.

I relegated it to the place of one-time slips and kept on as if it hadn't happened. Spent the money from it quickly and without thought. Spent the money that same night and went back to my day job in the morning. Parked behind the store like I'd been doing ever since I took this job.

All along I'd parked there instead of at the station. I was doing this to avoid going backward. I knew it couldn't last forever. Though, by this, I don't mean some dark character flaw on my part, or even the events of the night before, but instead something as mundane as the town parking-violations bureau.

This is the way things worked: the parking behind the store was free and for customers. It served the whole general shopping area, so you weren't supposed to park there all day long. What you were supposed to do was park at the station, which had twelve-hour meters for commuters and workers.

Getting caught cheating this setup was inevitable. After a while they would recognize your car. I'd already lasted longer than I'd ever expected. But that I got nailed this same morning? Well, it was hard not to take it as fate, or futility, I'm not sure which. In any case it made it hard not to make more of it than it was. And unlike the woman with the bad hip who worked in greeting cards, I certainly couldn't explain my particular reason and then ask for an exemption. So here I was back to walking across the street after work.

I didn't tell Beth this, but then I had never told her of my parking scheme in the first place. I guess I thought she'd think I was dumb for trying to protect myself this way. I guess I thought I was dumb. And because I thought my solution dumb, or that I was dumb for needing it, I didn't acknowledge that its end represented a risk.

I got caught midweek so I had the rest of it to practice walking across the street after work and driving to Beth's office. Then I had to contend with Saturday. I hated working Saturdays so that first week when I called in sick I didn't need to pinpoint what specifically I was avoiding. A whole other week went by before I needed to know that.

I expect you'll think I'm making a lot out of nothing, but after work that next weekend I had some difficulty. Of course, the Saturday train station crowd is a little different than the Monday-through-Friday guys. Different enough not to be there at six, my quitting time. What I used to do was go have a drink in that same bar adjacent to the lot.

So that's what I did this night, too. I went in and had a drink. Not right at the bar, but at a table close by. I sat there and watched the door pretty keenly, hoping and dreading I'd see someone. Hoping, I realized pretty soon, that I'd see Ingrid's husband and this both surprised me and didn't at all.

The guy who wound up joining me was named Burt. He said he thought we knew each other but I knew we didn't. He said he was a friend of that bartender I sort of saw for a while. I had to admit that was possible—them being friends, not his having met me before.

Burt seemed okay. Not what I usually gravitate toward, but okay. He asked did I want to go for a drive and I said why not, still not sure what he meant, or how we were talking.

His car was big and a soft shade of red and not new, but I was too out of it to think, Cool or Classic, I just thought, Old. The guy at the wheel had apparently been waiting there this whole time. Burt and I got in the back and that was that. We were off on the drive.

His house was a pretty long way away, though I still knew the area, was still on fairly familiar ground. He was having a party I guess because there were people on the lawn and more in the house. One guy headed for us as soon as we came in. He handed Burt a drink and they whispered and then he was gone again.

"Anything you need," Burt said to me, "Jeremy'll get it."

"Which one?" I asked and he pointed his glass after the same guy, though he was no longer in sight. I guess I should say right up front that I found Jeremy more than attractive. I found myself scanning the crowd for him. And when Burt had business in the bedroom, Jeremy sat me down on a couch. Told the guy who'd driven the car to bring me a drink.

Before I'd had even a taste of it I was thinking too much about Jeremy and in the wrong ways. He, meanwhile, seemed anxious for me to understand that he and Burt were partners. That he held a much different position than the other guys running around.

Sitting with him and talking was okay. But I assumed sex was why I was here, and so when that part kept not happening I got edgy. I think that's why I wound up staying so long. And besides I didn't have my own car or enough cash for a taxi. Picking up some extra cash had been most of the point, and now Jeremy mixed in with this too.

It had gotten late by the time Burt called me into the bedroom. The traffic in and out of there had been pretty steady and obvious. He offered the coke and I did it. It wasn't the best stuff but he had a lot of it. I figured there were other things he could get.

These reasons were enough for me to go with them to another house, which was somewhere even farther away. And while I make it sound like I had all this in hand, I didn't. Not really. I'd become nervous about getting home. And more nervous about the sex that still wasn't happening because if that wasn't the point of me being with them, then what the hell was?

At this house, Burt stayed in one bedroom on the phone, leaving Jeremy and me alone in another. The same driver was stuck outside again, waiting. Anyway, the two of us sprawled on the bed, curled up with a full-length mirror Jeremy had taken off the wall. We just did coke and did coke, and every so often I'd traipse across the hall and check in on Burt.

The first couple of times, I got on the bed with him. I sort of crawled up toward him, trying to figure out what he wanted. I got nowhere with this. Finally I took to just peering in from the hall, did it just to have a break from the other room where the only thing going on was the coke.

By the time it turned daylight I had trouble making it across the hall. I would have to sit down and rest. I would sort of fall down and stay there. This was a day I was supposed to go to that job. A day I was supposed to see Beth. I didn't see how either of those things would be happening.

Jeremy said he'd call in for me. I knew this would look worse than me calling myself. But I couldn't imagine doing it so instead of seeing it as crazy, I was grateful. He told them I'd gotten sick while spending the weekend at his house. He told me not to worry. That they'd sounded concerned. Of course, his perceptions by then were probably on par with mine, meaning off.

Not too long after this, when we'd gone back to what we'd been doing for hours, Jeremy said, "So, my guess is your bill's up to about a thousand dollars."

I froze when he said this, becoming cold and unable to speak. He said, "You didn't think all this was free, did you?"

He smiled that smile he had on his face almost all night. It reminded me how handsome he was, and also how large, physically. Reminded me he took up more than his share of the bed and that I didn't have a way home.

I hadn't heard Burt but he stood at the doorway. His voice was what pulled my eyes there. "He's kidding," Burt said.

And while I regained some of my faculties I still wasn't at all sure I believed him. And if they weren't after sex, then what? Because it just couldn't be as simple as money.

I never quite got myself calmed down. Jeremy made that same joke a couple of more times. And then there was all the coke. I was jagged from that. And still nobody'd laid a hand on me. There'd been talk about the three of us together. But even the talk didn't go far. No one could focus long enough. Then they'd dropped me at home.

Once in my apartment I started searching in coat pockets and drawers. I told myself I was only wanting equilibrium, wanting to even myself out. Not wanting to get off and go away from things. I did finally find a scrap of foil so small I had to put it on a pin to try and smoke it. I had to hold the pin with needlenose pliers. I lit the thing over and over. Sucked at it even when there wasn't any hint of smoke coming off it.

I wanted sleep, long sleep. And I wanted some chocolate milk. I used to always have some in the fridge. It used to help lull me. But now I didn't buy it anymore, not on a regular basis. I'd meant to quit this time. I'd also meant to call Beth. Reminded myself of this right before I finally dozed off.

Seventeen

It wound up that Beth called me. I was in that place of half-coked and dazed. That place where you memorize the ceiling but aren't quite conscious.

She said, "Where are you?"

It seemed such a silly question that I said, "What?"

"You're supposed to be here," she said.

And even though I got it by now, I said, "Where?"

She didn't say anything, and I didn't want her to think I was jerking her, so I said, "Sorry. Look, I'll come over now."

I hung up the phone and pulled on some clothes. And while I knew I looked bad, I still figured I'd pass. I was glad I lived within walking distance of her office because I didn't think I could drive.

On my way down the stairs, I considered taking my car any-way—it'd get me there that much quicker. But I realized I didn't exactly know where I'd left it. Then I remembered the train sta-tion. I figured it'd have a ticket lounging on the windshield. That people at work might notice, if any of them had noticed me at all.

So I walked. And it settled me down some, though it pumped me up, too. Woke me up. I thought I was okay by the time I got to her office. Though, really, I suppose I must've been kind of a mess.

If I go by the look on Beth's face, anyway. A look you'd call wary or guarded, or maybe simply confused.

I did my normal walkabout. She just waited it out. Neither of us talked and the silence finally sat me down.

"What happened?" she said. "What's going on?"

I started badly. I said, "I'm sick, is all. My stomach's upset and so I took the day off and fell asleep."

"Come on," she said. "Why are you making up stories?"

It was true I'd kind of forgotten who I was talking to. But at the same time I knew I had a reason for evading her. I couldn't place it, though. I couldn't remember back to the last time I saw her or what had gone on between us.

I stalled by not answering. Used simple silence. She leaned forward in her chair, rested her arms on her knees and clasped her hands. And when she spoke, she made her voice very soft. She said, "Please tell me what's going on."

When she talked to me like that, with that little catch in her voice, I could never defend myself. Before I knew it I was telling her. I was saying, "I got mixed up in something over the weekend and it stretched out. I couldn't get home and I couldn't get to work. And I guess I couldn't get here either."

"What, what did you get mixed up with?"

By now I'd recovered myself enough to see where I was headed. There was probation to worry about. And how much could I tell her without stretching her thin. I said, "Is what I say really between us?"

"It's that bad?"

"No. Maybe it's not as bad as all that."

"I think you better tell me."

"Who do you tell then?"

"No one. I don't tell anyone."

I considered this a moment. I don't know if I believed her. What made me go on was realizing nothing had happened. I hadn't sold any sex and while I'd done drugs, that wasn't prohibited; well, that's not what was spelled out in my release agreement. It wasn't a condition. Drugs hadn't even come up. It had been all about hooking. And so what could they get me on now? Intent to commit prostitution? I didn't think so.

So I made up my mind just to go ahead and talk, but I still had trouble starting. I'd left out too many things along the way. Things I wished I'd said because it'd make this easier to explain and just plain shorter. I wanted to start from the beginning but as I searched back for that, my brain grogged out while my body sharpened.

The way I was sitting hurt all of a sudden so I uncrossed my legs. Before I knew it I was rubbing my thighs, trying to get the pins out. I stayed in the chair, though. I considered this an accomplishment. And eventually I stopped my hands, stopped them moving, but I couldn't let go of my legs. It seemed if I did I wouldn't know where I was.

Beth didn't say anything about any of this. When I looked at her, she'd sunk back in her chair and was watching my hands. We both seemed to have lost any sense of time. I'm not sure she knew where to go any more than I did.

I only knew not to make a run for the door, though I couldn't say why. And my hands on my legs, instead of stopping the tingling they absorbed more and more of it until it traveled up my arms. I rolled up my sleeves, made small tight folds that stopped just above my elbows, thought this could tourniquet me off, keep my chest clear anyway.

"Why don't you tell me," she said finally, and it was a suggestion, not a question, so it seemed a way in.

I told her the events without filling in what went on behind them. I didn't say I was looking for money, didn't say much at all about Burt or Jeremy. I kept it to drugs, and a party that dragged out, and not having a ride home.

Beth said, "You know, you need to hang on to that job."

"Yeah, I know," I said.

She said, "No, really. It matters."

I knew she was talking legalities but I also knew the probation was pretty short. That I'd be free of it in a matter of months. I didn't care about keeping the job, not beyond the absolute minimum to be practical. But I saw what had happened by having left so much out, and so how could I blame her for choosing the wrong tack in all this?

Unless I gave her more to go on I knew she couldn't help much. I crossed my arms and hugged my chest because despite all my efforts the quivering had found its way there.

"Are you cold?" she asked.

"No, not exactly."

She leaned forward again, clasped her hands again. What she said was, "I think we need to talk about Ingrid."

This I didn't expect. I found myself clutching my chest even tighter until I let go altogether and instead tried to breathe. Breathing worked better.

She still sat that same way. She looked at her own hands now, not mine, and I thought I saw something sad, but shifty, going on in her eyes.

"Why Ingrid?" I asked.

"Because she's where we keep stopping."

Beth still watched her hands. What she said was the truth, but not all of it. What she wasn't saying—that's what made me tell her, and so my reasons weren't much better than hers. I wanted to get her going, wanted to upset her so I started hard. "So, you want to know how we fucked, or maybe how much, or how about where?"

She acted as if I hadn't put it this way. She said, "I want to know what you need to tell me."

I said, "Well, I want to know what you need me to say. Or how about why?"

I stopped myself here. I could see what I was doing. The corner I'd backed into felt almost homey.

I needed to decide why I was stalling so badly on this. I mean, sure, I could put it on her and why she wanted to know. And her reasons not being stellar made this all the more tempting. But it still fit much too neatly with my need not to talk about this.

Beth and I would get where we were headed whether I told her about Ingrid or not. This I already knew but chose not to acknowledge. If anything, I could've used Beth's intentions as incentive. Let them egg me on as a kind of reward. The kick was I could only actually see it that way if I thought it wouldn't happen. And lately, who knew?

And Ingrid? To see what happened with her made me feel dumb and run over. Like all the time I'd spent so worried about her husband was wasted because it left me wide open to her. And then she'd hit me so hard I barely noticed.

You understand, right? How I could land on my back and just lie there? From that position, it's hard to make sense of things. Hard not to get caught up in someone telling you the things you've wanted to hear your whole life, and so does it matter if what they're saying is true? In that moment, I mean? Does it matter?

I'm not saying Ingrid lied. I know she believed the things she said if only because she had to. How in hell else could she possibly see me as a way out? That piece had always been pretty hard to swallow, but it gave her a push. And me? Not much else was asked but to be who she needed me to be, which was exactly the thing I'd been born to.

This wasn't the stuff I planned to tell Beth. I'd keep that to what she wanted to hear because like I said I'd been born and bred that way and it's a hard thing to break out of. Besides, breaking me out wasn't something either of us was up to, or planned on—maybe not ever and surely not right now.

Beth had let my last question hang, the one about why she wanted to know. She looked hurt about it and I couldn't decide whether to lay off or go in for the kill. "Never mind," I said, trying to pick a place in between. "Never mind. I think I know why."

After I'd said it I realized it could mean anything. And the way I'd said it, which was sort of gently, anyone'd think …

"What is it you think I should tell you?" I said this gently too because now that I'd started this way, and almost by accident, a pull had begun and I couldn't resist it. It was all I could do to keep from actually comforting her. By this I mean getting up and putting my arms around her.

"Why don't you just start where it starts," she said, and she sounded so weary.

It wasn't until then I realized I hadn't said any of it. That I'd stayed with stories about harmless commuters and any time I got near Ingrid and her husband I circled back. Not quite—I mean I had told her about my first time with him. I was pretty sure of that. Well, not entirely, but pretty close to certain.

"Did I tell you about going back to the house?"

She shook her head rather than speaking and looked out the window. It was too dark out there to see anything and soon she got up and pulled the shade. When she sat down again, she looked at me. I realized what I should've done was go to her at the window. This would've been a way out except I'd missed it, been too slow on the uptake.

"I never went home with any of them. It never entered my skull and none of them asked. They were all hiding from home."

I carried on this way for a bit, making the important discovery that I could stall and talk at the same time. I could probably keep it going for hours and never get to the door of Ingrid's house.

I don't know why I didn't do it that way, but instead I found myself getting to the point and kind of quickly. Began telling her about sitting on their couch with Ingrid's head in my lap and him behind her.

Something about telling this was catching me up. So much so I didn't look too close at what was happening to Beth. Instead I watched the small crack of blackness at the bottom of the window shade—the place where it almost hit the sill but didn't.

I noticed, by chance really, that she'd focused over my shoulder. And though it wasn't something I'd ever done before, I stood up and went to the other window, the one behind me. I pulled that shade down.

I guess I knew it was an invitation. She must've known too but she didn't take it, and so I stood there until I felt foolish for standing. Now that I felt weak like this, she got up and came over. She stood near me, first without touching and then she took my hand.

It could've been she'd heard enough. Or maybe that I'd become lost and foggy. She just stood there holding my hand and if I wanted a way out it was right there before me. I'd come to understand that when we went that route, I'd have to start it. That she'd need it that way. That it was the one thing she couldn't quite do.

But I couldn't do it either. Not right now. Not with the last few days catching up to me. And not stuck right smack in the midst of that first time with Ingrid. That was where Beth had left me. I suppose this was why I shook loose from her and went to the door, and maybe, too, it's why she didn't stop me.

I just walked out and kept walking. I walked until I got to the train station. My idea had been to pick up my car. And I did. I picked up some cash on the way, did a couple of guys on their way home from the bar. Just blow jobs. I guess this time I'd been looking to. I guess I'd been looking to since Friday.

Eighteen

I went back to work the next day. My day job. Though I guess I went back to the other thing, too, and for a while it kept being harmless. I couldn't pick up the guys right off the train and still get to Beth's on time, so what I started doing was heading over to the station afterward. Getting the guys coming out of the bar. And while their being drunk made some of them easier and more generous, it made others nastier. Impatient and impotent—this combination I seemed to encounter more and more often until I got nasty back and then got off on it.

I was working this fine. It made more sense all around. And it gave me something to look to while I sat with Beth and tried to answer her questions. It distracted me and I used the distraction to keep her at bay. I even convinced myself she didn't notice the change. Or that if she did, like me, she saw it was for the better.

The money helped, too. Though it started that same calculation in my head. The "Why am I keeping this stupid job?" I suppose I was keeping it for Beth—because to quit would give her something to latch on to and worry about, give her a distraction. I suppose I was keeping it because of what happened the last time I quit.

I still looked for him, for Ingrid's husband. I knew he probably wouldn't turn up. And I knew I wasn't looking for him in the right way. I wasn't anxious and fearful of an encounter but instead longed for one. I couldn't conveniently file this, couldn't make it about getting to Ingrid. It was about that, but not only. What I'd had with her had been so vested in him—so in relation—that when she got free of him, even if only in theory, there wasn't much left between us.

I figured they'd found someone else by now. Someone closer to home or farther away. Maybe they went to her, or to a hotel. Maybe she was younger and easier, or older and more of a pro. I still had a lot to learn about indifference.

Despite knowing all this I kept looking for him but the one I kept finding was Burt. By comparison, he seemed a lightweight. Someone I could easily handle and therefore, I guess, boring. The hold here was drugs—coke, the promise of junk, an occasional Quaalude. I couldn't conceive he was playing me and so I didn't worry much along those lines. He was something to do at the end of a night. Someone I didn't have to do and so, if my body could rest, he could fuck my mind all he wanted.

That's what Beth seemed to be doing, too. Every afternoon like the last one, sitting in her office while she tinkered and I kept remote. We went on this way some weeks before she said, "What is it with you?"

It was her voice, the bite in it that made me sit up a little. Cross my legs one way, then put them back the way they'd been all along. I looked at my watch, trying not to make it obvious. The crowd I usually caught would be starting out of the bar about now.

"You have someplace you'd rather be?" she asked.

This seemed an odd way to put it, plainer than she'd been lately. It made it easier. "I've got a night job," I said as if she might not know what I meant. As if she were dumb.

She didn't say anything right away. Looked unsurprised but maybe deflated. This led me to fill space.

"It's not like before," I said. "It's nothing dicey."

"Do you want to get arrested? Is that it?"

"I never would've if he hadn't set me up. They don't care what goes on there."

We didn't take it much further than this. She let me leave a little bit later but I didn't go to the station. I told myself it was too late to catch enough action.

Instead I drove around. I drove until I found myself cruising back and forth past Ingrid's driveway. I even drove a little way up toward the house. I was looking for lights, but I knew I wouldn't go in. I wasn't sure whose house it was now. I couldn't tell just by looking because nothing had changed. This was the idea I went home with.

Two nights later I was back hitting the parking lot. I'd just done a guy, just gotten out of his car, when I saw her car—Beth's—stopped at a light that had already turned green. She was looking my way, but looking at me? I couldn't tell. I could practically convince myself it wasn't her. That I couldn't be sure.

The next afternoon I was sure. She didn't say anything about it but she looked at me differently. Like what she hadn't believed before, not entirely, was suddenly true and made her mad. That's what I thought at first, until she said, "Let's go for a drive."

We'd never done this before and so I got into her car wondering what she expected of me. Was I supposed to put my head in her lap? Was that what she wanted? Or was this simply her way of keeping me out of other people's cars?

She drove us around for a while and then up a long driveway, one that started out paved and then turned to dirt. When we got a certain way up, there was a bend. From there if we went any farther someone would see us so she turned off onto the grass. She parked there and I knew she wanted something but she wasn't saying what it was. She took my hands in hers and then began talking about how I worried her and what was I doing, why was I doing it?

I couldn't answer her. Not just because I didn't know how to, but because of how she was. Because of the force of her hands on mine and the look in her eyes and the sound of her voice, which was desperate. I wanted out of her grasp, out of her car, but that'd leave me standing in the middle of somebody's field and then too I didn't think it would solve anything.

I knew Beth wouldn't just leave. I tried to remember if there'd ever been a time I'd wanted to get away from her. If it'd happened before, this feeling I mean, exactly this one.

What I did, because nothing else seemed possible, I just sat there. I hoped that if I could just manage to stay in the car we'd keep things contained.

I waited it out, saying nothing. This bothered her, got her more rattled. And we might've sat there forever except this guy came across the field. He looked every part the hillbilly protecting his land except he had no gun in his arms. It took me a moment to be sure of this.

He told us to get off his land. Beth went beyond flustered trying to explain who she was and what we were doing except it seemed she didn't know either and he absolutely didn't want to hear it. He said he knew exactly what she was and what we were doing and that he didn't want us doing it on his land.

I smiled. I couldn't help it because what he was driving at was so obvious and it was a relief to have it spoken. And then too I was angry at her and felt some power in watching her scramble, in hearing this total stranger say out loud what she and I had been playing with for months.

What could she do then besides start the car? She didn't say anything driving back and I sure didn't and so this became a thing we never mentioned—something that had happened between us but that we'd never speak of. And not the first of its kind.

Nineteen

This didn't put her off taking me driving, it only made her choose more carefully where to go. Since public places and someone else's backyard or field or driveway were out, what she did was take me to her house. I don't remember how it happened we went there, what her reason was, though I think it had to do with her picking up something to take back to the office.

I went in with her. Edged around the corners of her rooms, not sure where to put myself, whether to follow her or not. This wasn't conventional, even for us, and so I wasn't sure of the etiquette. Still, when she went upstairs I went with her, and from there we went into the bedroom.

I wandered around in there. Picked up stuff from the bureau. Looked at the pictures. Just being in there but not quite invited, I felt like the one in charge.

Pretty soon, though, she was saying we should go. I don't know what she'd been doing or pretending to do. I mean, it wasn't like she'd found what she came for and so wanted to leave. She seemed hurried and off like the day before—addled—and this made me bolder. It made her easier to get at. So I was the one who lingered. The one who wanted to stay. Or at least acted like it.

I was standing near the bureau and she came up behind me and

She could tell, I think, because she kept saying for me to let myself. Instead I pulled away from her. I kind of crawled away and then was kneeling with my back to her. She was on the bed behind me and she'd pulled my shirt off my shoulders. She kissed me there, and my neck, all the while murmuring to me in this way I loved and wanted more of but didn't trust, in this way I wanted so badly to give in to, but kept fighting.

She kept talking softly, and her arm around me, her hand moving from my stomach to my chest and then lower and back up to my throat, at first this was what held me up, what helped me. Her hand, not what she was saying.

With her mouth so close to my ear I could hear every word but couldn't hold on to any of it. The things she said worried me most, scared me most. Scared me for her.

I'd kept hold of my shirt. I'd kept my elbows bent so she couldn't take it all the way off me. But now I let my arms drop back behind me because I needed us to get to the next place we were going. Needed this because I thought it would stop her from talking this way.

Once she had my shirt off, I had nothing on anymore and neither did she and this seemed to be what let us lie down together. I was on my stomach and she was behind me with one hand inside me and the other holding me around my waist. I could only make sounds and do what she wanted me to do, which was pull one leg up under me more.

Her hand in me had me near begging her. I felt crazed in a way I didn't know, or could barely remember. Crazed and swallowed somewhere and then coming up again and then not anymore. Just staying down there, staying with her and when I'd gotten to this place, she took her hand out and put it in my ass and then I was begging again. For real and out loud. Begging for more of her. Asking from this place in me that felt early, as in ancient, but still very young.

I was pleading with her and she kept telling me to let myself. She kept saying, "Sweetheart, let yourself have it."

And her telling me this fastened me to her voice, to the sound of it, which was so gentle and knowing. So convinced about what would make me feel better. That the way to this was through giving in to her, to what she was saying.

I could listen to her now because the words were about what she wanted from me, what she wanted me to do, and not how she felt, so I could be with her. I could be so close to her that she became who I most wanted her to be. For a little while she did. Until I did what she told me and let myself come.

Once that happened, the shift in me was so fast I thought I'd go under forever. This rage came up and over me with such fierceness and sorrow I feared I'd turn on her. But then instead of it swallowing me, I swallowed it. And before I understood any of it, I'd begun all the motions of loving her back.

I got caught in this fast because it let me feel all those other things again. The first and most important of these was being turned on, the only one able to drown out the others. Or permit them. The one that allowed me to feel things I otherwise never felt safe with.

But then all that was over too. And she seemed so at peace in my arms while I felt in pieces and wanting badly for her to notice except she didn't, and so I was left alone in my head where nothing good was happening.

All of this felt familiar and strange. It had something to do with how I managed the men, but in another way it had nothing to do with all that because the men didn't start this trouble, the women did. And not even all of them, and never anyone had like this, like Beth.

Ingrid had begun it, had come closest. She'd shown me myself and where I was headed. She'd made it clear I couldn't keep on with what I'd been doing. That it didn't matter anymore how hard I tried, I wouldn't be able to keep the things inside me where I thought they belonged. That it was only a matter of time and maybe of place before I lost hold.

Until Ingrid, I hadn't felt anything in such a very long while. I'd made sure of this. I'd promised myself. My life may have looked haphazard and I suppose a lot of it was, but I'd kept this one piece very well ordered. And even with Ingrid I'd seemed able to keep myself under control.

But not with Beth. Since the first day I laid eyes on her I'd been fighting myself and then just plain pretending. Had done this by seeing what I felt for her in one way only. Had tried to make it just about sex, but then that was what led me here. What put me in her bed where feeling became suddenly everything until the feelings themselves overlapped and tangled up, impossible to distinguish, or stop, or recover from.

These were the feelings that had made it necessary to stop feeling in the first place—necessary to stop all of them. Or at least dull them, blunt them. Find so many ways around them, to never allow them. To keep myself especially far from love and even further from being loved because, of the whole lot of them, these were the only two that could actually kill you.

All this crowded into me while Beth slept in my arms. And it made me panicky and flighty. Restless enough to get up and put on my shirt and my pants and then search out my cigarettes, which were caught in the sheets near her feet. I found myself wanting to wake her, wanting to shake her awake, and I did jostle the bed more than I needed but she was sleeping too deeply to notice.

And because I understood so well this kind of sleep and how impossible it is to intrude upon, I went down the stairs and into the living room, curled myself into the far corner of the couch and smoked, wondering what day it was going to be and what it was I was supposed to do. I did this until she came down the stairs with my shoes in one hand and my socks in another.

She handed them to me and I put them on—all this without a word passing between us. And we said nothing putting on our coats or the whole way in her car. And nothing still when she dropped me at my car.

Twenty

It was still dark when I got into my own bed and by then I knew which day it was turning into, and knew I'd call in sick to work. And I was sick, I supposed—and with the whole weekend looming.

I spent the day in bed nursing a loneliness too large to ignore. A lovesick that wouldn't let me alone. This was the place I called her from and so I wasn't in my right mind.

When she answered the phone, she behaved warily, needed coercing and cajoling. This just left me feeling sicker about all of it, and more to blame. She agreed to meet me not on this day but the next—Sunday—at her office.

By the time I got off the phone it was early evening and dark out so I could feel at least that I'd gotten through the worst of the day and partway into night. And going by me fast and unfocused was a thought about heading for that parking lot.

I went no further with this because meeting her tomorrow held me a little together, while at the same time letting me know how pulled apart I'd become. That it wasn't really peace of mind keeping me at home, but the belief I was so fractured I could actually be in danger, or put myself there.

This wasn't something that occurred to me often and, even now, recognizing it was only surface. Pure practicality and going no deeper and so absent of true understanding. It would keep me safe though—as in at home for this night—but could effect no lasting change or even begin it.

I had nothing in the house but booze and this situation almost sent me outdoors after all. The realization I didn't know anyone who could get me anything better stopped me. And it let me know that if I was going to stay with Beth that would need to change.

The way all this went reminded me none of it was new. But placing its origin—placing this at my origins—tired me so much I got a tall glass and began drinking. Did this until I found a place of comfort nothing could intrude upon, though just before I slept I thought of Beth sound asleep and this troubled me until it soothed me instead.

The next morning my head hurt too much to lift but this wasn't the drinking. Drinking never did this to me. I forced myself out of bed and through the motions of morning, though it was already a little past noon.

I had about enough time to get myself together before I'd meet her. I winced some remembering that phone call. Now, seeing her seemed a very bad idea but still impossible to resist.

I got myself dressed, and then I put on my coat. Noticing it was the one she'd loaned me, or given me—that helped not at all. So I walked over there already angry and beholden.

She'd gotten there before me so I just walked through the waiting room and into her office. It seemed odd to be back here. The room seemed too small to hold us and I couldn't tell if she noticed any of this because she just sat there as if I'd been keeping her. As if I was late, but I knew I wasn't.

I did my weekday thing of being unable to sit down, only it seemed worse and all about not looking at her. Still, the pressure to just get on with this was somehow even greater. I slinked, I truly did. In a very animal way I slid into that chair.

Her body let go a little once I sat down. I didn't see this so much as feel it. I did notice she'd uncrossed her legs, let them fall just a little apart. But seeing what I was looking at made me meet her eyes.

She appeared just as wary as I was, but at the same time letting go to this unfounded faith. Or maybe this last thing was just happening to me. In any case I couldn't hold on to my body at all anymore. My limbs fell into the chair very loose and heavy and pleasant. I rested my head and closed my eyes and then I heard her come toward me.

I kept my eyes closed because this seemed the best way to handle things. She'd knelt before me, had started with her arms around me and her head resting against my chest and then my stomach. She just sort of held on to me and I didn't know what to do. What to do in return.

I'd had my hands on my thighs but now I put the right one, which seemed easier to lift, on her neck. I kind of rubbed her neck and I couldn't get past thinking this should be the other way around. That I should be on my knees to her. But that was not how it was.

Soon the same panicky flight thing began in my chest and I couldn't believe she didn't feel it in me. But maybe she did because she started rubbing one of my thighs with one of her hands and that made it all easier.

I opened my legs more and I wanted so much to gather her into my legs and my arms, hold her with all of my body, but this sort of thing was clearly beyond me.

Instead I just kept falling backward, loosening myself and loafing. Letting her do it all. She'd opened my shirt and my pants, had done all of this so slowly I couldn't place when it had happened. Only knew that now her hands were on my skin and so was her mouth.

She stayed very slow, eased my pants down but left my underwear. She kept touching me so lightly I thought this by itself might kill me.

I'd become very quiet. My breathing had dropped so far down. Nothing about me was awake except the places she touched. From here I cared only for physical comfort. I kicked off my shoes and shucked my pants and underwear. I was glad I'd never put socks on because when I wrapped my legs around her I especially liked having the velvety feel of her blouse against my feet.

The sensation of this held me a little while but then her mouth took me over and I clutched her hands first and then her arms, pulled her into me and me into her.

I'd gone to that place where nothing mattered but her and how she was making me feel. With this hitting me so hard, I wanted something more than a chair underneath me. I wanted maybe to be on the floor except it would've involved too much movement. It maybe would've spoiled something and so I stayed put, recognizing that possibly what I wanted was to crawl away from her again.

What I did instead was hold her even tighter, grasp her with my hands and my legs. The pressure of this helped me in a purely physical way. It spread the shivering that had fixed in my chest through the rest of me and this let me stay with her. Stay with what she was doing to me, which was bringing me toward feelings for her I could just barely take and then bringing me off.

From there we did wind up on the floor. And me, I was weighted with all the same tangled mess—that same too-strong love, turning in an instant to fury. I didn't take her clothes off, only took down her underwear and hitched up her skirt. I did the least I could do to get my hand into her.

She made sounds as I fucked her. All of it was so fast and so rough, so the back of what she'd done to me. I feared I might actually hurt her.

But afterward, she held on to me and was kissing me and saying those same kinds of things I couldn't listen to. I found myself reaching for my pants and pulling them on. Seeing this as the way to be able to stay next to her and hear her.

Once I'd dressed I found myself undressing her, pulling her skirt off first and then her blouse. I still needed something to do in order to listen.

She kept on talking. It seemed to come from some dreamed place inside her I didn't yet know and because of this feared. I stroked her body. Her belly and her thighs, her throat. I kissed her shoulders and breasts.

These were things I'd been unable to accomplish the other night. And maybe she'd missed them because she left off talking. I heard just her breathing. I felt it go low, and then I felt her lower. She sort of murmured something and I kept my hand soft. I brought my face near hers, surprising myself because I wanted to know what she'd said.

She didn't say it again though, and my mouth was so near hers, still, what I did was bring my hand to it. I ran my finger along her lips and when she opened her mouth to this, I kissed her. This was where I got lost again. I caught myself lolling. I'd rolled off her a little and she onto me and so what I needed to do was regain my balance.

I shifted my weight so we were back where we'd been. I had to fight myself to stay slow. I put my hand down on her while I took my mouth away. She made those same sounds. Small cries that caught in her throat before they grew heavy, and by then she'd gone someplace she didn't come back from.

I couldn't wait for her. The room was too small and her holding me so tight cluttered me. I pulled away. Put my shoes on and left her there. I left her lying on the floor.

Once out the door I didn't go back the way I came. I turned the other direction, which took me nowhere but out of my way. I walked and walked around the early evening of this town where nothing ever happened. I walked quite a ways along one side of the main street before turning and heading back toward my place, which meant passing her office.

I told myself I wouldn't look for lights or her car but of course I did. Saw the car but not the lights. The same as I had that other night. My thought was, What if I've killed her?

I didn't know where this came from and so I shook it away and then felt only tired. I was relieved when I saw that pharmacy with the neon drugs sign reminding me I was home.

I climbed the stairs and my legs felt so heavy I had the urge to reach down and lift them.

I knew it was Sunday, this was the one thing I was crisply aware of, so much so it hurt me. And while it was still pretty early I couldn't imagine ever getting enough sleep. Ever getting enough sleep ever again. This seemed something she'd taken from me. Or something she'd made me see I'd never had.

Twenty-One

So I went to work the next day because, after all, I only seemed ever to go one or maybe two places. I went through the whole day reminding myself I had the next day off, and telling myself I'd skip seeing Beth.

Still, around three, I took my afternoon break at that bar. I fueled up, and so I expected not seeing Beth was another promise to myself I wouldn't be keeping.

I'd left off using my car. I suppose I mistrusted myself with heavy machinery. Anyway, I'd left it at home and so after work I walked there, to her office, and this meant I was late.

She was in the waiting room. Waiting. Actually, she paced. But when we went into her office I did the pacing, though not for long at all, which seemed curious to me. She seemed curious to me too, the way she acted.

She was asking me questions the same as before. What struck me was how long it'd been since I'd heard her voice—in her conventional role, I mean. Saturday on the phone stood out. Other than that she'd spoken only in that way I couldn't quite grasp because it stayed too far inside her.

I realized quickly that I couldn't make sense of this voice either—the everyday one. It was too thin. It gave nothing to hold on to. Whole phrases went by me and I answered none of her questions, which was at first unintentional.

Soon, though, a disgust grew in me and with it an obstinacy when I understood what she was doing, that her intent was to proceed as if yesterday hadn't happened, or the other night either. And while I grew angrier, disbelieving and impatient, I could not contradict her—this was the card she held. And either her recognition of it or my behavior made her nasty.

Little by little she began to taunt me, to poke at the silence that had become my lone weapon. If I couldn't say what she was ignoring, it looked like I would say nothing at all. But then quickly I told myself this wasn't about principles. Not for me. What upset me was simply not getting the gratification I'd come for, and ascribing anything more was merely false and indulgent.

It was true I'd assumed we'd just keep on. That it would be all we would do. And so now her trying to backtrack? I wanted none of it. And I hated her for it, and hated even more how I still wanted her despite it.

From here I could see nothing to do but walk out. Maybe I thought she'd follow me or stop me. That then we would wind up where I wanted to be. But she did neither.

I would've gone to the parking lot but I didn't feel dressed for it, or up to it. I simply went home and once there I drank and drank until the phone rang and while I knew it would be her, still it surprised me.

She said she only wanted to know was I okay and I told her sure I was. I told her this sullen and cross like I wanted her to go away but please not to. She stayed on the phone with me a long time and soon it became clear this was to be the bridge. The place where we'd talk in halfways and circles. The way for her to reel me back in, and for me to let her.

Even her voice was somewhere in between and she played me and played with me until I'd begun playing with myself, let her hear me come close to coming. And I heard things in her that maybe were the same—changes in her breathing, only her breathing. Gaps.

I liked this too much. Already I could see what it did to me. That no matter what it might seem like, or be like, always I'd be the one on my knees.

For a little while though I could make believe she was the one who'd come crawling to me.

Seeing things this way got me through the night and into the next day, which was my day off. Somehow our game on the phone tired me more than anything so far. This particular languor made me reluctant to attempt even the simplest things. I puttered around my apartment. Killed time. Killed the day until it was time to go to her office.

I suppose I'd expected that after the phone call we'd wind up next to each other again, close. But this wasn't what happened. She kept her distance and it annoyed me. It annoyed me especially when she suggested that at least on Tuesdays, when I didn't work, I come see her earlier. "During my regular hours"—that was the phrase she used.

This made me sick and angry all at once but I stayed silent, acquiesced by inaction, and consequently she had her way again. I stayed silent pretty much the whole time. She seemed so relieved to have made her one point and won that she didn't even try to get past me. We put up with each other, I guess, and then I left.

This uneasy balancing kept on for the rest of the week, leaving me swamped and achy. Despair I think is what you would call the thing getting in the way of everyday tasks like walking and eating. But on Friday all of it changed again without warning. She changed. Or maybe it was me, unable to keep my pose any longer. Maybe my face gave away my grief, or maybe it had all week long and I'd only now worn her down.

I'd been staring over her shoulder, as I had been for days, when some small movement of hers caught my glance. She was holding her hand out to me and I was slow and out of practice but I took it.

This was not the most comfortable position for either of us, stretched between these two chairs. They seemed actually farther from each other than they used to be. We were still in a battle of wills. I understood that this time it should be me who went to her, and I both wanted to and couldn't.

I wanted very much to make it easier for both of us, but I couldn't move. This wasn't about stubbornness or anything resembling it, this was just deadness. A deadness I couldn't shake or force myself through, and so I wasn't forcing her either. It seemed closer to pleading, though without words.

I suppose all the significant things between us happened this way—silently, or at least without speech. That I was speechless again at this moment felt nearly ordinary. Like a thing I was used to, or the thing I was most used to.

She seemed unable to wait any longer. She pulled me to my feet, and I fell against her with all the same deadness. I could do nothing but lean.

It felt better like this. I felt better. But at the same time I believed I'd given in. This seemed backward to me and so I had trouble following it. I didn't see how I should feel this defeated. I thought maybe she should.

She was holding me kind of loosely. She stroked the back of my neck, and her fingers underneath my hair and running through it let me rest my head on her shoulder. She kissed my neck and murmured to me the same way, so softly and gently. And if she was using words I recognized them only as sounds.

She kept on this way and the urge I felt was to cry. To finally let myself do this because it seemed I'd needed to for a very long time. But having no knowledge of what I would be crying about stopped me. It bewildered me to feel something so strongly but without content. Unnerved me so, I wanted to pull away from her. Blame her for starting this unsettled thing roaming through me. Maybe I thought getting away from her would stop it.

I must have made some small move in this direction because she tightened her hold, assumed a knowing firmness she seemed to reserve for my moments of doubt. I couldn't help wanting actual words telling me things were all right. But I recognized it was too early for this.

I concentrated very hard on her hands—where they were and what they were doing—because unless I did this I couldn't remain standing. Now that she was moving toward what I'd wanted, I needed things to stay this way. Stay soft and sweet and aimless. Now I wanted to backtrack. And though this had been what she'd wanted, it seemed something we couldn't want at the same time.

Still, where things went wasn't specific. It could never be that simple thing again of touching and comfort. But recognizing this meant seeing it never had been like that—mindless and guileless and building blindly somewhere.

Part of my deepest trouble was knowing we'd known. Knowing she had. I couldn't keep this in mind and keep food down, or keep on my feet. And just from knowing this much for this long, my stomach went swimming and my head, too, fell underwater, and so I landed in another of those floundering stupors.

I knew what happened for her in these moments, that they were the ones she waited for. Fending off this knowledge took stamina, though, the last of mine I suppose, because I could no longer fend her off—if I'd ever been trying to or able.

She'd gotten both her hands under my shirt, was stroking my back, and I found myself unzipping her dress. From here I became nearly aggressive. That she seemed to want me this way, like me this way, does nothing, ever, to ease me.

I took her to the floor and took her dress off, and the rest of her things. Then I fucked her. It brought me out of my daze and into some kind of command and it had everything to do with rescuing myself. It had nothing to do with giving her pleasure.

That it had something to do with that for her, with pleasure, only confused me and so returned me to where I'd begun. Gave the game back to her, gave me back to her. I lay beside her, still fully dressed but out of my head again, which meant inside my body. And the things going on there, as usual, distressed me.

Because of this I didn't try anymore to affect what she did. I found myself looking up at her because she was on top of me now and looking down. This tormented me so completely but I couldn't see why. I only knew I couldn't get my breath and that to try to made this sound—a kind of sound I didn't want anyone to hear.

I tried to throw her off me, go back to where we'd just been, but I couldn't do this or anything else but lie there gasping.

She unbuttoned my shirt, which frightened me more. I tried again to kick her off me but my legs stayed as useless as the rest of me. She was running her fingers right down the middle of me. She began at my throat and stopped each time at my waist. I thought she'd maybe smothered me because I became very lightheaded. My breath couldn't follow her fingers, couldn't go below the place she touched on my throat.

She didn't stop, though. Instead she did this again and again.

And then there wasn't lightness in my head anymore but heaviness. I let it rest on the floor, only then knowing I'd been craning my neck the whole time.

Once I let my head go the rest of me followed. She kept up the same way and I began to find comfort in it. Began not to want her ever to stop or go further.

For a while it did stay this way. And I could let my breathing follow her fingers. I was breathing into my belly and not caring by now if I watched her. And I didn't care when she unbuttoned my pants. I told myself I didn't at all.

I helped her undress me and once we'd done this she seemed to know to go back, to keep with what she'd been doing. I lay there the same way, and we were just as we'd been, except now she was kneeling. She had her knees between my legs and so it was plain that this place we were in wouldn't last very long.

I did my best to stay there regardless, stay with the comfort and not go beyond it. To keep to my body, keeping my mind at bay. And so when her fingers began to drift that bit farther down, each time it helped me. And what I felt when she began saying things? It was all about wanting her close to me. Wishing myself able to hear and believe her.

I had this need to hold her. I tried to prop myself up in order to do this. But I didn't get very far and what she did was put her hand inside me. I felt her other arm go around my back and hold me up a short while before she leaned into me. Then we were both lying down and I was grasping at her and at anything else that might anchor me.

Her mouth was close to mine and she kissed me. Her tongue took up so much room, left me wordless and hers. She let her hand come out of me. Did this as I came. Both her arms wrapped around me and I held on to her, too, and this kissing felt like all anyone could ever want or ever could need.

It was all that we did now. And it seemed to go on forever, until it stopped. Then, even with her there and still stroking my face, it was over too soon. And none of it felt like enough. And maybe not to her either because the restlessness didn't seem mine alone.

Pretty soon both of us were on our feet and staggering around looking for our clothes and clumsy in putting them on. And then, like always, we seemed so much further away from each other. Like maybe we didn't know who we were, or who the other one was. Or who we'd just been.

After she got dressed, Beth sat down. She stared out the window and I stared at her until it made me want to go to her and I knew I'd better leave. Still, I lingered. Stood there stupidly with my coat in my hand. I think I was waiting for her to say something.

She did but, while it was what I should've expected, it wasn't what I wanted to hear. She said, "I think you'd better leave now." And her voice sounded flat and emotionless like it did each time she uttered these particular words.

She wouldn't look at me, which was true of the other times too, but this was the only time I'd wondered about her end. Saw it as anything other than disgust for me. Saw it as maybe my having some effect on her. That the things she evoked in me might be roused somewhere in her.

Thinking this way kept me standing there, and I was afraid for her to look at me. Afraid for her, and of her, and of standing there long enough to want her again, or feel wanted by her instead of cast out and alone.

Twenty-Two

I got out of there. I went directly home, and once there tried not to think of the only thing I could think of, which was when could I have her again.

It'd been a Friday, so I should've been going to work in the morning. I knew this much, though it didn't mean I'd do anything about it.

When the time came, I called in sick, not remembering until afterward that I'd done this same thing the week before. I realized maybe I ought to begin worrying what they would think. I already didn't make enough there and I hadn't been making money any other way lately. Something needed to change.

I lay in bed and tried to convince myself Beth only meant trouble. That the thing to do was get away from her. Some part of me knew this completely. But thinking about leaving her left me thinking about her. And once I'd begun that, the will to leave her didn't last long.

I told myself I had to keep seeing her. That it was merely practical. I tried to reorder my need, make it about legalities. This was so thin even I could see through it. Still I worked hard to stay on this plane. Not drift into thinking about how she could make me feel, when she wanted to, which didn't seem often enough.

I couldn't face calling her. Spent the day—Saturday—avoiding this impulse. Finally went out to avoid it because I couldn't stand that she might play cool and aloof and impossible. That this weekend might completely match the last one, with me ordering myself around her, running to her and not knowing how I'd find her. I already had this sense that she took up too much of my life, or maybe all of it. And right when I needed badly for this not to be true I ran into Burt.

This was not a hard thing to do. It was only a matter of going to certain places at certain times. And so I did these things believing I had no plan in mind. He was at that bar, with Jeremy. And I'd seen his car in the lot with the same guy waiting behind the wheel.

They sat me down at their table. Began buying me drinks and all through this I had that same nagging sense of wondering just what they wanted me for. They weren't talking to me really, not exactly. I was just there listening to them. Then they got up and we all went out and they gave me a ride home, which was good since I still wasn't driving my car.

This put me pretty much where I'd been, only later and drunk. My resolve was nowhere and so eventually I found myself calling her. She sounded sleepy and irritable and not quite surprised, so I couldn't help feeling she'd won.

I didn't ask to see her. Not asking felt like the only way I could preserve some kind of pride. This seemed to confuse her, and since I hadn't called with anything else in mind we stumbled around for a while with her finally saying, "Why don't you meet me at noon."

She said it in that in-between way. We'd slipped back to that. Fallen back into playing each other. Playing with each other and ourselves. And it almost made me say where and, besides, her office seemed too small and not right. But we didn't say any more, and I went to sleep feeling, well, happy's not quite the word but secure maybe. Drunk anyway.

I woke up later than I'd intended and with that same sense of having made a mistake. I thought quite seriously of standing her up. Really wanted to, but the motive was flimsy, hard to determine, harder to act on.

I arrived at her office disheveled and discouraged. She'd gotten there already. She came out to the waiting room and took my arm in a way that reminded me we hadn't always been like this. From here we went into her room and sat down. I felt oddly comforted and it made me unsure what I wanted from her. She seemed that way too—tentative, different than she'd been in a long while.

I didn't say anything but found myself looking at her intently. Meeting her eyes for what seemed like ages. When she spoke, when she said, "Are you all right these days?" the sound of her voice startled me.

I didn't know how she meant this. How widely she meant it. How much ground I was allowed to cover if I answered. The easy thing would've been to say, Yes, I'm fine, but this was so far from true I couldn't shape the words. What I said instead was, "I don't really think so."

I looked at her when I said it and wished I hadn't because it seemed to have hurt her. She maybe wanted the other answer. How could I know what she wanted? "Are you?"

Her face changed again. She looked like she had no idea what I'd said and so quickly I added, "All right, I mean."

Her eyes went cloudy and then teared and my own vision blurred from these same things, and we just sat there staring at each other.

I wondered about the way through this, how to come out the other side and quickly. But just when I thought I couldn't stand this another moment, it grew sweet. Like we shared something, even if it wasn't a good thing. And I felt a type of closeness I hadn't felt in what had to be months.

And while this took over my body, while this sweetness roamed my chest and then the rest of me, taking hold in my limbs, I willed my brain to keep out of it, to stay still and not to wreck it, not to start me pumping to leave or push this into sex because those escapes were there too—always there and calling.

She didn't fidget, and she didn't look away. But she didn't say anything either. Not for the longest time. And then finally what she said was, "I'm afraid I'm not helping you."

I couldn't imagine how she meant this. I wanted to laugh, but she seemed genuine. Seemed not to see the absurdity of what she'd just said. This left me lightheaded, nearly giddy, unsure I could keep hold of what seemed maybe like anger.

There was so much room here for nastiness, for sarcasm. The only thing stopping me was the look on her face, still truthful and gentle. To meet that with cruelty seemed wrong. Instead, I said, "How do you mean?" And I truly wanted to know because the eeriest thing was the way I could never tell if she acknowledged all of what went on between us.

"I mean, I think you're getting into trouble."

I wondered if she was talking about herself more than me, if she meant I was getting her into trouble, because now her eyes left mine and stared out the window until this began to feel like all the other times she'd tried to keep herself away from me.

"How?" I asked her.

"You're going back to it."

"Not really, not that much. Not lately."

"Weren't you just last night?"

This threw me. And when her eyes met mine, they looked sore, achy. I tried to see what she'd said in some other way than that she'd gone looking for me.

At first I thought she'd maybe seen my car in the parking lot. Made her conclusions from there. But then I realized I hadn't been using it and so what did that mean? That she'd actually been in that bar last night?

"I tried calling you," she said. "I wanted to see if you were okay. I hadn't heard from you. I was worried, and so I went by your place but there were no lights, and you didn't answer but your car was there."

Her eyes drifted away and when she started again, she said, "I saw you at the train station. With those men."

She said all of this like it made sense. Like it was the most ordinary thing for a person to do, and it was hard not to go along with her. Not to feel that yes, of course, she's the one who knows what she's doing.

I kept my head just above water. I said, "What is it you think you saw?"

"I saw you get in a car with them."

I wanted her to look at me because all I could see was her sitting in her car, watching for me. I couldn't stand what this had me wondering and it made me plainer than usual. I said, "Look at me."

But when she did she seemed to almost be crying and so I looked away.

I said, "So you imagined the rest of it."

"Should I have stayed and watched?"

I wanted to say, What were you doing there in the first place? But this gave me too much to sort through. I felt both unnerved and afraid of her, and at the same time cared for—that she would go to such lengths, but out of what?

"They drove me home."

"Oh, and that's better?"

"No, that's it. That's all of it."

I said this not quite understanding how quickly I'd become the one defending my actions. It served both of us, though. Let her stay above question and let me avoid thinking what the questions should be.

I stole a look at her and then another. And when I could be sure she'd gotten hold of herself I kept looking. This put us back to staring at each other, which started hard and almost mean before it went gauzy. I wouldn't touch her. I kept telling myself this over and over in my head until I believed it, but I began to see leaving as the only way to ensure it. I thought, This time might really hurt.

So I did leave, and she didn't stop me.

I went home to find something I never could have expected. Inside my building, just outside my door, Ingrid was sitting on the stairs. The way she looked—so lonesome, so much like I felt—it took away any will I'd ever had with her. And with Beth at my back, the sight of Ingrid felt like relief.

We went inside and she stayed standing near the door. She sort of hovered there like she didn't know any better than me why she'd come. I put down my keys. I took off my shoes without thinking because my feet hurt, unaccustomed to so much walking.

I sat on the couch and waited. Ingrid finally sat down, but on the edge, keeping her coat on. She acted confused—with me or herself, I couldn't know. Something looked even more wrong than usual. This made me reach over and pull her coat from her shoulders and then pull her toward me. I held on to her while she cried. I kissed her hair and held her.

I didn't think I wanted to know what had happened—what on earth could've put it in her head to come here. I knew we'd wind up in the bedroom but I hoped it would take a while because I was afraid of what I might find on her body.

It was bruises, all along her left side. The kind you get from someone getting you down on the floor and kicking. She never said how. She never explained it. But then I suppose that's what I offered—someone she could go to without explanation. Someone who'd simply know and know exactly.

We didn't really do anything more than lie around with each other. Finally I went to find some ice. Being only as far away as the kitchen gave me the distance to wonder what jeopardy she'd put me in by coming here. And if she began making a habit of it? This appealed to me even as it frightened me.

I went back to her. Laid a towel on her side and then the ice and then put some pillows around her. All of this began me thinking about the way it had been in their house. Her having done this kind of thing for me. And I began to feel I owed her this. That she would do the same for me. That she already had.

Twenty-Three

In the morning, I had trouble with Ingrid even being there. I got up, took the towel away, now soggy and cold. I did these things trying not to wake her and she went along with this. She seemed dead to anything I might do and I was glad for it.

I needed time by myself. I needed at least to figure out what day it was and where I should be. It felt like Sunday but knowing it wasn't did nothing to put me in motion.

It was late enough that the phone began ringing and I knew it'd be someone from work trying to find me. That was about the last thing I could see dealing with, so I unplugged the phone. I decided right then I wouldn't go back to that job.

This meant having the day with Ingrid. Maybe it did. After all I didn't know her plans. How long she expected to stay. I'd remained in between not wanting her there and feeling closed in, but at the same time afraid of her leaving, not for her but for me. Afraid of being alone with myself in a way that might make me look at the things I was doing.

Ingrid did stay. She spent the day in bed, not really ever awake. I waited on the couch, realizing finally that what I was missing were my afternoon drinks, the ones that usually started at lunch. I pulled out a bottle and a glass and lay there drinking awhile, watching Ingrid through the bedroom door.

About when I was getting dressed to go see Beth, Ingrid got up and went into the bathroom. After a while I heard water running. I heard what sounded like her getting into the tub and I went in to brush my teeth.

"I have to go out for a little bit," I told her. And though she looked stricken, she must've pulled herself back from this because her voice was steady when she said, "Would it be all right for me to stay here a few days?"

I considered this, knowing I would never refuse. But that alone couldn't keep me from considering just where this would put me. Would she stay here while I went back to work for real in that parking lot? It would increase the chances of her husband showing up, looking for me. Or sending someone else to do it.

"You can stay as long as you need … As long as you want." This was what I finally told her. And when I began my walk to Beth's I noticed my car parked in the little lot by my building. I wondered if I should move it, put it somewhere else. Whether it would be something that would tip Ingrid's husband all the faster to our whereabouts. But, of course, I knew he'd find us easily whenever he bothered to try.

I got to Beth's office still edgy and distracted. I couldn't tell how she was. It seemed forever since I'd seen her, what with all that had come in between. She looked different to me, but then she did look different during the week. More distant and composed, if only on the surface.

"You didn't go to work again."

She said this as a statement of fact. I was still standing, running my fingers over a glass paperweight full of trapped, dead flowers.

This object sat on her desk, which meant I stood right behind her. Something I'd never done before while walking around.

She didn't turn to look at me when she talked. Instead she looked straight ahead and at the chair I should've been sitting in. Having Ingrid in my home gave me some kind of false something. I guess bravado because I felt less like I needed Beth. Though I suppose I needed her more. If only she'd ever been someone I could talk to.

I'd moved so quickly to the other side of what I'd just been feeling. Began feeling so swiftly small and afraid, so in need, that I did sit down and when I did I astonished myself. I said, "I think I'm in trouble."

She looked at me. She said, "Tell me what's happened."

I had enough sense to know I couldn't do that, not exactly. I said, "I can't go back to that job. There's some way I just can't. There's too much else ..."

I expected a lecture. Something standard she'd shift into from habit. Instead she said, "Do you want to do the other thing more?"

"No, I don't think so. I don't know. I just know I can't play store any longer. I don't belong there. I don't know who I am there because I'm never there, not really, not me."

"You belong where?"

"I don't know. Maybe the other thing suits me better. It's all clearer."

I didn't know why I was saying these things to her and I believed I'd better stop because it seemed dangerous. She seemed dangerous if I let on what really happened inside me.

I waited for her to argue with me but she didn't, she said, "Why do you think that?"

"Because I know what to do, what's expected of me." And then I thought of Burt and said, "Most of the time, anyway."

I sat there unable to say anything more. I gazed at her, while longing seeped into every space in my body. It gave me a strange solid feel, but with a weight to it. A weight so heavy I couldn't have gotten to my feet if I tried. But she was on hers, holding her hand out to me. And then I was standing and we were walking out to her car. She had her arm around my waist and I was leaning against her, and now the heaviness of my body felt pleasant.

She drove us to a park near her house. No one much was there, it being later than dusk and cold out. I pulled at the coat she'd given me, drew it close. It was odd to be among swings and slides, things children play on. The cold air felt good, though. And she felt good, still with her arm around me, still guiding me. The sweet sadness of this made me want to cry. And then before I'd registered wanting this I'd already begun it. Had begun to cry from that place so big and so old I didn't know where it began or what it concerned.

I cried in her arms for what seemed like ages. And when I couldn't stand up anymore, we sat on a picnic table. We sat there timelessly, me gathered up in her arms and still sobbing. Then I'd stopped, or it had stopped, all this crying. And she'd moved us back to her car and there we were inside it. But this had happened too quickly. So quickly, I wanted her to turn down the street to her house. She didn't. Instead, she drove me home.

My place did make more sense, what with her having a husband. But then here I was with someone else's wife, so what could I do? She said, "Will you be all right? Do you want me to come in with you?"

Of course I did. I wanted her more in that moment than maybe I ever had. Though how I wanted her? I couldn't be sure of this, except to know it wasn't the same. Pieces of it were but the whole of it wasn't.

And Ingrid upstairs? I couldn't tell Beth about that. There was nothing to do. I said, "No, I'll be okay. I'm all right." And then I said, "Thanks." And before I got out of the car I put my arms around her neck and held on for a little bit. And when I went up my stairs I felt nearly okay. For a little while.

Ingrid was on the couch and dressed. She looked like a wife all of a sudden. She'd fixed us dinner somehow or bought it somewhere. We ate and had some drinks and it began to seem normal to have her there. And though I'm not proud of it, it crossed my mind she might take care of money for a while. Postpone my having to go out again.

We were drinking still and smoking when the phone rang. And my instinct was not to answer, except for knowing it was Beth.

I picked it up and she said, "I just wanted to make sure you're all right."

I walked the phone into the bedroom, closed the door to Ingrid, but I still couldn't shift gears so fast. I felt the jerky guiltiness in my voice when I said, "I'm okay, really." And everything about the way I was speaking made plain my impatience. She couldn't know why, just sounded sort of confused, and what she wound up saying was, "Tomorrow, why don't you come later than we said."

"When?"

"Six, I guess. That would be better I think. I have a full day and …"

She didn't bother to finish, as if she remembered who she was talking to.

"Six is fine," I said. "I have some things to do, too," and I didn't know why I said this last thing and wished I hadn't.

"Oh," she said. "All right. Six, then." And I felt her lingering and it felt brutish to edge toward hanging up, but in another awful way it seemed to be working in my favor.

"Okay, I'll see you then," I said.

I hung up the phone and went back to Ingrid. She still sat on the couch, smoking a cigarette, staring at her drink on the coffee table.

"Who was that?" she said like she'd had years of practice, which of course she had.

It startled us both. Her more than me because she quickly said, "I'm sorry. I don't know why I asked that. It's none of my business."

I didn't attempt to explain, though a part of me wanted to. Here I was again with all this inside me I wanted to say but with the absolute wrong person to tell it to.

Instead I held out my hand and she took it. We went into the bedroom, me not knowing who or what I wanted exactly. I only knew too clearly it was Beth who'd started me needing and then changed the shape of the need.

Ingrid and I lay down together. It seemed at first that it might be like last night, with us just lying around. And, in a strange way, recognizing this—that this might be what I most wanted from Beth, or would've tonight—drove me past it. I couldn't lie there thinking about her, about Beth. If I did it might start me crying again. Crying from that place I didn't understand, and that'd give Ingrid all the wrong sorts of ideas about me. I'd be the last thing she'd want.

I undressed her and then undressed myself and she turned the covers down. She must've made the bed. I stood there, wondering at what I was doing. Not just this minute but with the whole of my life. Wondering how in hell I'd come here and from where.

These thoughts must've stopped me entirely because I heard Ingrid's voice. Heard her say, "Nina, what is it? What's the matter?"

I discovered myself standing stock still by the bed, but breathing hard, wishing I'd told her my real name because maybe then I would've felt like we knew each other.

"Nothing," I said as I got into bed with her. But it wasn't going to work. I could tell this already. I couldn't get rid of all the things I was thinking. And when she began to touch me, at first just my neck, stroking a line under my jaw, I knew I'd never keep from feeling things either. And so with neither my mind nor my body a safe place to be, I looked to her body. Turned toward her and began touching her in return, and for a short while this worked.

I began to kiss her shoulders and then her breasts. Did these things until all I felt was her and not me. And this lasted until I pulled the covers back, saw the bruises on her side, by now purple and still reddish.

The sight of them caught me up, nearly stopped me. For an instant it ran through my mind to ask how it had happened. But I knew this, too, was about me, about keeping me from myself. And I knew it wouldn't work. Besides, I knew exactly how she'd come to be hurt in this way. I could see it all—her on the floor and him kicking her. And I knew that the times I'd had this done to me I'd felt the least human of all.

To make her revisit it just to spare myself, this seemed close to something he'd do. Instead I put a pillow behind her so she wouldn't have to lie flat. She sank into it while I wrapped my arm around her thigh.

I kissed her forever, her belly, her thighs, and I could feel her hands in my hair. Could hear her saying little things. Murmuring in a way I couldn't make out and didn't quite want to—afraid it might sound too much like what Beth said. And if they were both saying the same kinds of things, how could I believe either one of them? How could it be any more than the things people say when they're together like this? And this was made all the more tangled by my wanting to believe Beth but not Ingrid.

So, in this way, I came back to Beth just as I got inside Ingrid. I listened to Ingrid now because it was only sounds and breath, and my own breathing changed but not in the right way. I had to take my mouth from her, and just fuck her. Fuck her, while I tried to choke off my own sounds because they might end up in sobs if I didn't get hold of myself.

Ingrid tried to turn—first toward her bruises but crying out some when that hurt, and so toward me. I pulled out another pillow. Let her onto her stomach. I got myself up and behind her. Put my hand back inside her, and her asking all this time now for more of me, of my hand.

I grew afraid of myself in this, afraid I'd get carried away, carried off to where she wanted me to go and then I stopped worrying.

I fucked her until she was the one crying—out of a place I both knew and didn't because usually when she got here she stayed silent and away from me. But this time, when I was starting to stop, she cried at me to keep on. She said, "Please, don't. Please don't leave me."

She'd never said anything like this and so I listened. I put my hand farther into her and held it there, kept trying to get farther inside. She held herself very still, and then I did this, too—I held still and held my hand still, still and deep.

I stayed like this until she turned again. Turned toward me, and her face looked a way I'd never seen. She looked young and afraid and I opened my arms and she came to me.

It was a long time before she quieted. I felt helpless. I thought of all the stupid things to do—bring her a drink, a cigarette. I kept myself from doing these things until she got to a place of wanting me to. Then I was glad to have actual tasks. To be able to get up from that bed.

I brought these things back with me—the bottle, our glasses. Made a separate trip for the cigarettes just to have more time with myself. I tried to drink the way she did, in the long swallows that were helping her, but for me it just brought back the choking. And the cigarette I tried did this, too, even more. I stubbed it out halfway finished, and that's when she noticed me.

She curled up near me and put her hand between my legs and I lay back. I opened my legs because she told me to.

She stroked me and stroked me and I felt a calmness begin near her hand and then follow it. She trailed her fingers up my body to my throat and back down. Beth had done this too, and so I wondered: What is it about me that lets women know to do this?

My breathing grew steadier and deeper and she talked to me in a way that said nothing. She said things like, "There, now. You're all right. Darling, everything's all right." And I could see that it wasn't, because I'd begun to believe her.

When she put her hand in me I couldn't be anywhere else but with her. I couldn't do anything but feel what she was doing. And it was all slow and gentle and I wanted more of her than I could take. Tried hard to ask for her but now I was the one who could only make sounds and cries.

She knew anyway. We were enough alike in these ways and so I felt her get very far into me and felt myself close around her. I wanted to put my legs around her, too, but I couldn't move them. I felt limp and wonderfully exhausted, slack and peaceful. She seemed to find comfort in this because when I looked she was smiling. Not in any large way, but this small change in her face that I hadn't seen in a long while, maybe ever.

She took her hand from me slowly, let it stay underneath her when she sank into me. And I felt her hand and the weight of her body as indistinguishable things. And I came in this way, too. A way that made it hard to make out what was what, and harder to care because all that seemed to matter right now was her having had me this way.

But it didn't last. It went wrong because she wasn't the right one to have done this, to have done me this way, done this to me. And so from underneath came an emptiness. Seeping through me, despite my attempts to keep it away. It nagged me. Gnawed from inside, forcing me to see Ingrid and I weren't so very alike, or weren't anymore. What still worked for her seemed now to fail me. Couldn't keep pace with what Beth had begun—something that seemed unstoppable, yet might never finish. Or might finish me.

Twenty-Four

I slept, really slept deeply, for the first time in longer than I could determine. Still, I woke uneasy again. Felt nervous of Ingrid, and having her here. I was glad it was late. Glad there was less of the day to face. Glad that it was only a few hours until I'd see Beth because, in the backward way I have of thinking, I thought she'd help me sort out something I'd never mention to her.

I wanted to feign sleep, let Ingrid get up first and she did seem to be awake, though I didn't exactly want to know for sure. I had my back to her because, the way we were arranged, her bruises gave her just one way to sleep, which was facing me.

I could feel her body shifting, first in little ways and then she ran her fingers down my back, slipped her leg between mine. It seemed she'd woken to where we'd gone to sleep. I envied her this, wondered how she could manage it. But as I took her hand and pulled her arm around me and felt her mouth on my neck, I realized this was maybe only escape.

Once I'd gotten to this, I couldn't lie there any longer. If I did I'd see all of last night in this one way only and I needed it to mean more than that. At least for a while I needed it to because I was the one who'd begun from that place. Who'd needed to escape myself, the place Beth had taken me. That old place awash with sorrow.

No matter how hard I wanted to, or pretended to, I couldn't use Beth for escape. I'd never been able to. What she offered was its opposite. She plunged me into the very things I'd needed to get away from. Swamped me with them through the same means I'd always used to evade them.

Sex with her wasn't only sex. Not in the way I'd known it for so long. With her it became something else entirely. Something she knew so much better than I did. And her knowing more of this thing I thought I was expert at forced me to see I'd only known its most insignificant pieces. That for as long as I'd let myself remember, I'd kept it to these little bits.

Thinking this way got me to the kitchen and smoking and making coffee, having my first cup there without Ingrid. I brought her hers trying not to think that this mimicked how we'd been at their house. I was tired of the way we couldn't get beyond the things that had happened there, and that these things still happened to her.

She let me alone. But when I got back into bed I felt her looking for a way in and it pressed down on me. It made me want out—out of the bed, out of the apartment. Made me know I had only the one place to go and not yet.

The day kept awkward like this. The two of us not saying much, doing less. And me trying to keep from the one way we knew each other. She tried to get us back there a few more times, but I wouldn't let her. I didn't know until I was on my way to Beth's that my reluctance was about her and not Ingrid. Or about both of them.

In truth, Ingrid had never let me escape myself either. She'd begun this, started disabling my mechanisms. Not the way Beth had, but by being so like me I couldn't not see myself. I'd seen myself in her. Seen all the holes in my system—in me—and how apparent they were to anyone who cared to notice. And Beth? She'd been the one who'd noticed, whether I'd been ready for her or not.

I went into her office with this still in my mind. It kept me wary. Kept me from looking at her even longer than usual, and kept me on my feet even longer. She waited me out.

When I finally sat down, I let myself look at her. And soon as I did something large and quiet took me over. The looseness of my body made me want to tell her all about Ingrid. But at the same time it made speaking feel too far away. And it seemed my hearing was off too because when she spoke to me, I barely noticed.

"What?" I asked. And I wondered how long it had taken me.

"Who was with you last night?"

She said it without emotion. But the complete flatness of her voice made clear how hard she was working to keep it that way. At first I thought she somehow knew everything already. I nearly proceeded that way, but my general slowness let her be the one to say what came next.

"I don't think you should bring them home with you."

Now her voice wasn't so steady and this and what she said gave me a direction to take.

I said, "So you're convinced those are the only people who'd come to my house?"

My voice stayed even through this, but I wasn't trying. It was this thing still inside me—this quiet that had hold of my limbs and seemed to be running the rest of me.

"I'm saying it might be dangerous."

I had no clue how to play this. The urge was there, to tell her about Ingrid, to use her as a weapon. Instead I said, "I've never done that."

"Then who was it?"

"No one. All right? Who else is there?"

We were still looking at each other. Her face had colored. She didn't seem to know what to do with her hands. I surprised myself by getting up and walking toward her. I took one of her hands and, when she didn't get up, looked too startled to, I crouched down. Was on my knees to her. And then, feeling out of my skull, I began kissing her hand. I did this until she let it open.

I pressed her palm against my cheek. Held it there for a little while until I was kissing it again, sucking her fingers. She didn't move for the longest time. Then her knees, which had begun firm together, loosened, let me closer. I put my other hand under her skirt. Ran it up her thigh to where her stockings ended. And just for a moment I found myself wondering if she'd always worn stockings or if this, too, had something to do with me.

I couldn't think this way for very long, so instead I listened for her breathing. I tucked my hand in back of her, pulled her close to me and laid my head in her lap. I had my other arm around her, too, but outside her clothes. She'd begun stroking my face and I closed my eyes and simply held on.

We stayed this way for some time—not speaking, not moving too much. Finally she said, "Come on, let me take you home."

I knew what she meant and wished it was that easy. Wanted her in my bed more than I could ever remember wanting anything, except her, and just last night, just this way. To have to say no, to have to invent some way around it, felt like more than I could manage.

What I said was, "All right." And we got to our feet and got pulled together. We got ourselves outside and into her car. And I believed that between here and there, in those five minutes, I'd figure something out.

I didn't and, of course, she could feel me trying to. She kept asking me what was wrong. And then she pulled into the little lot by my place instead of up at the curb. From here, so clearly, you could see my lights on and I watched her noticing this. Ingrid might as well have been standing in the window.

Beth faltered but, true to herself, she continued as if she'd seen nothing. She said, "Let me come in with you." And when this must've seemed too plain, she quickly added, "I want to make sure you're all right."

We'd gone again to that horrible place of pretending who we were to each other. Or she had. My head in her lap a few minutes ago and now it was simply about concern. It gave me the push I needed, though. I said, "I'm fine. You don't need to worry about me." And this came too quick and too sharp and she looked stung.

"Look," I said gentler, trying to patch things. "I'll see you tomorrow."

She just sat there with her hands on the wheel and this strange look on her face. She still stared up at my window.

I got out and walked around and into the building. Climbed the stairs two at a time. Ingrid met me at the door. She said, "You've been gone a long time."

This sounded odd to me, out of place. It made me wonder how much I could tell her when maybe it should've clued me somewhere else. Still, I liked her hands on me and her arms around me, and then I could play her game a little longer. Could see what she said as just nice. Simply about missing me and wanting me because after all she'd been cooped up here all day. I wondered how much longer she'd be able to stand it.

She pulled me toward the bedroom but I broke away, said I'd be there in a minute. I went to the window, knowing I hadn't heard

Beth's car pull away. Hoping I was wrong and knowing I wasn't, I stood away from the window and pulled the shade. And then I went to bed with Ingrid, knowing I had to find some way to get her out of my place.

Twenty-Five

The next morning I decided it could be simpler than I was making it. That maybe Ingrid only needed to leave for an evening. I approached this while we were still in bed, having coffee.

I said, "I need to entertain someone. Just for tonight."

She acted surprised and not surprised, all at once. She said, "If it's money … You know I have money."

"It's that, but not only. I quit my job. I can't just keep on like this."

"Like what?" she said, and it sounded close to pouting.

I didn't say anything, and she caught herself. She said, "Well, I really should be getting back to my life."

I didn't know if she meant this to hurt me the way it did. And then before I knew I had, I'd said, "I don't want you going back to him."

"If I don't, he'll come looking. I'm surprised he hasn't already. I suppose he knows where to find me."

I pulled the covers up because I felt cold as soon as she said this. And seeing me, she said, "He won't come for you if I go home. I've taken too long already."

We didn't say any more about it and so later, when I left for Beth's office, I didn't know for sure what Ingrid would do. I puzzled this my whole way over there, still worried about it by the time I was sitting down and facing Beth again.

She looked almost as if last night hadn't happened. Almost. Something in her maybe couldn't keep all the angles going either. But that didn't change things much.

She said, "I'm worried about you not working."

This was how she started. It annoyed me, her going back here. For this reason alone I said, "Oh, I'm working."

It was an ugly thing to say and I wished I hadn't. I knew I was holding Beth accountable for Ingrid going home, for what she was going home to, even. And I knew what was really to blame were my feelings for her, for Beth. I blamed them for everything—their largeness, the way I could never put them away but always, always had to do something about them.

Beth stared out the window. She wouldn't look at me even when I began trying to mend things. I started lamely, saying, "I didn't mean that. It's not even true."

This last bit seemed futile. I knew she'd think I was lying. And then too, maybe what I'd been doing with Ingrid wasn't really so different, was really just the same kind of work.

"There's just one, anyway," I said, lumbering on. "Someone you don't have to worry about."

She glared at me. "Do you think I'm stupid, or do you believe that yourself?"

This was so unlike her, it stopped me. And maybe it was the truth in it. That somehow, once again, I'd forgotten to see how things were with Ingrid—the jeopardy involved, which was certainly more than with any commuter.

"No," I said, cowed now. "I suppose I don't."

I would've said whatever she wanted if only I could figure out what it was. I would've said it and even tried to mean it. "What do you really want from me?" This was what I finally asked and it wasn't mean. I meant it as an actual question and this softened her.

"I don't know," she said, and her eyes wavered, drifted to the window before they came back to me.

We sat a long time this way, saying nothing until I felt the silence under my skin making me twitchy. And so finally, just to stop this feeling, I said, "Would you take me home now?"

She didn't say anything. She just got up, got her coat and we were out the door and into her car.

She pulled into the lot again. Glanced up at my darkened window and then back at me. She wasn't going to ask again, not tonight, I could tell. So I said, "Would you come in with me?"

Again she said nothing. She just got out of the car. Did this before I had. We went around to the door and up the stairs, and this whole time I feared Ingrid might still be there, asleep maybe, or something.

Beth stood behind me when I opened the door. And as soon as I saw the envelope—a fat one on the coffee table—I knew Ingrid was gone, maybe gone from me for good.

I hesitated, or maybe I went backward, or Beth kept going forward. Whichever way she was there, pressed up behind me, forcing me ahead.

I went in, turned on a light. I tried to pretend the envelope wasn't there. Beth stayed standing near the door. Her doing this reminded me she'd never been here before and that it wasn't normal that she was now. It was too forthright and obvious, too planned. Somehow I felt like the lone instigator.

I went to the coffee table because I couldn't not anymore. I didn't have the energy required for trying to hide things. I picked up the envelope. It wasn't sealed, it was too bulky. There inside—one twenty after another, some fifties, even hundreds near the back. No note, which I realized was what I was looking for, what I needed more than the money, or at least in addition to it.

I felt something go wrong inside me, so wrong it was physical. A nausea of sadness, making me need to get rid of the envelope because it seemed to have caused this. I went into the bedroom as if Beth weren't there. I didn't know right away if she'd followed or not, then knew she had.

I opened a drawer in a bedside table, tossed the envelope inside and slammed it. The noise of this echoed as I fell back on the bed. I leaned against the wall, pulled a pillow to my chest and held on. Beth stood in the doorway. She looked odd—framed there with the light from the other room creeping in, and this room so dark, always so dark.

"That's a lot of money," she said, very matter of fact, like she wasn't thinking, What did you do for all that? Except I knew it was what she was thinking. And more than that, Who did you do it for? This brought some new kind of fullness into my chest until I couldn't breathe with all the anger there. And somewhere underneath this anger was fear. The fear that Beth knew exactly who'd been in my bed.

What happened then rearranged things. She came into the room and sat beside me. I didn't know what I wanted from her anymore, or why she was here. I didn't know why wanting her had made me send Ingrid away. Especially I didn't know because in some big unformed way Ingrid was who I longed for right now. Though whether this came from guilt or desire I couldn't be sure.

Or maybe I did want Beth if only she'd behave the way Ingrid did. If only she'd just once make things clear and keep them that way. Not pretend they weren't happening. Not carve us up one day to the next. Not fuck my body one night and the next day make believe she only picked at my brain.

Beth took my hand, uncurled it from the pillow and held it in hers. She did nothing else for a long time. We just sat there with all these unspoken things pushing us first one way, then the other. Always winding up pushing us closer, except I didn't want to be there. I wouldn't go there this time. Not with this stuff simmering in my chest and then roiling.

I would've gotten up if I could've, but to do what? Calling Ingrid was on my mind, but there were so many things in the way of this. So many ways I could never do this, and these things making me want to. Letting me know I would. That it was only a matter of time.

Beth stayed very still. She still had her coat on and I realized I was still wearing mine. Realized how hot all this had made me—her coat on my body and my fury inside.

I pulled my hand from hers and took off the coat. Began unbuttoning my shirt only because I felt so heated, so closed in. I didn't see what this would say to her.

She saw. She put her hand on my chest, went to start that stroking game again. But her hand there only made me feel the thing underneath it more fully. The smoldering, festering thing in my chest, burning hotter and sore, blistering. And her fingers trying to cool it. Trying to draw me into that marshland of hers. That place that pretended to be an ocean or pool but was really a swamp. Thick and slippery with quick-mud.

I wouldn't let her. This time I would have none of it. Not her way. I grabbed her wrist and twisted until she cried out. I gave way a little and she regained herself.

She said, "Sweetheart, you're hurting me." Said this as if I'd made a mistake, as if I didn't know what I was doing.

I twisted harder again. I wanted her to know precisely what I was doing and why. I wanted her to see exactly what she was doing. I said, "Ask your fucking questions. Ask the thing you need to know."

I saw her face harden and sharpen. Watched her working a way out, an evasion. And I saw pain there. I twisted harder. I wanted to hear her cry out again, needed to, because it was the only place in her I'd believe.

I was yelling now, yelling, "Go on. Ask it. Or say it. I don't care which."

And when she did, it was both at once. And she was yelling when she said, "She was here. Wasn't she? It's been her the whole time. This whole time it's been Ingrid. So who've I been? Tell me that. Just another trick?"

"You're the one who can't decide. The one playing tricks all the time."

"Goddamn you," she said, and she pummeled my chest now. Loosening things there, breaking them up and apart. "You're the whore," she said, "not me."

And then she really went at me. Went after me with her fists. And her words still spilling everywhere. "You fucking little whore," she said half crying, half yelling. And so finally I was getting what I thought I wanted. I was getting the truth out of her. The truth I'd believed all along.

She was on top of me now, still in her coat. I scrambled to get some command, but she was too far ahead of me. Already she kissed me hard, in a bruising way that tore at my lips and my mouth. I wanted to hit her. I tried to hit her back, but she was too much in charge. And before long this felt good. It felt close to relief because right now I wanted someone beating me, and this seemed right—her being the one.

She got her hand into my jeans and then into me. She still yelled things. Was yelling, "Is this all you want? All you think I want?"

And she fucked hard and I gave way because the answer was yes. If I could've spoken, it would've been, and then I did. I said, "Yes," but I said it in that other way that means fuck me, keep fucking me.

She did. She kept on and kept on. And she kept saying things, angry things I had no trouble hearing. She said, "I'll fuck you sense-less, you ... Goddamn you."

She'd gotten me out of my clothes, and she'd taken off some of hers. And she'd gone out of her head, but I was still in mine and registering everything going on—in my head and my body and the place in between them. That place being nearest my chest, where I wanted to feel deadness or at least hatred but instead could only feel loved.

I felt this the way I knew it. It wasn't that place she'd brought me before—the one I needed so badly, and then right away needed out of. It wasn't that tangled-up thing, so gentle and soft and unbearable. The one I'd tried to turn into this so many times, every time.

And her words weren't those ones, the ones she'd used all along. She wasn't saying, "You don't know how I love you. How I want you. How long I've wanted you. You don't know what you mean." But I kept hearing this anyway, echoing back at me. I could hear this so clearly, so much clearer than all the times she'd actually said it.

And she'd been right to tell me I didn't know these things, couldn't possibly know. I knew the things she said this time. She was the one who didn't know what she was saying, or what she was doing. Her words had garbled with the strength of her hand. I couldn't tell them apart, she'd so thoroughly glommed me.

My eyes closed and her hand hit me deeper and harder. And the words hit this way too, each time getting further inside me. Now just three or four, over and over. Now just "Goddamn you," and "You fucking whore." Again and again.

I let her do what she needed. I let her wear herself out on me, and wear me out. Liking too much how it felt, how it hurt me. How it made it all clear. That, always, this had been where we were headed. Where I'd push us. The place I was supposed to take her. The way I was supposed to make her take me.

But underneath, there was an uneasiness. That this wasn't her after all, but who I needed her to be. Who I'd made her. I thought it was my job to show her herself.

I thought this was always my job—to make people see something ugly inside. Take them to a place in themselves they didn't want to go, but had to. Let them do this through me and then let them discard me, discount me. Later on, making them pay me, never seeing how I paid for this too.

So I'd applied this to Beth. Made believe I'd show her something in herself she didn't want to exist. Now this all seemed wrongheaded, about me so much more than her. Who I needed to see and not who she was, not entirely, not the whole of her. Not even most of her. And what if this was true of others?

The mistake I'd made, the mistake I was, only grew larger as I recovered my senses. She'd done just what she'd said she would do. She'd fucked me so far into senseless I didn't recognize myself coming back.

And I didn't recognize myself coming, only knew she'd finished me. Was maybe finished with me, and if that was true then I had nothing left.

I lay there spent, or expended. I went to a place of not knowing anything anymore, especially who I was, or always had been. So maybe I had got this all wrong, even backward. That Beth was the one making me see things inside, go places I didn't want to go, but had to. And what I found there wasn't ugly, not exactly. Messy and massive, monstrous even, but not evil, more a behemoth than a demon.

I stayed in a half sleep for what must've been hours. Stayed suspended somewhere. And I suppose she slept too, sort of, because then it was light out and she got up from the bed cursing herself, but no longer cursing me. Maybe she simply realized there was someplace else she needed to be, and hours ago.

She left hurriedly. I didn't know what I felt or how I felt but most of all I had this sense that whatever was inside me no longer mattered. That I'd forfeited all of that, forfeited mattering to her. I believed there'd be no point in ever going near her again.

And then I was sleeping some more. And the place I slept was endlessly black. Blank and empty before it gained substance. Before it consoled me in a way I remembered from somewhere as old as the place I'd gone in those times she'd loved me.

Then I was waking up again. And not wanting this, wanting so much to stay encompassed in darkness, this darkness, belonging only to me. But right away thinking at least I had that money. That it would buy me the time to work these things out—work out who I was now, or who I'd been all along.

I nearly expected Beth to have left money, feared maybe she had. That I'd find bills crumpled somewhere near me. But she hadn't done this so I could slip back to that darkness. And it pulled me back, encircled and held on. And I was clinging to it, not wanting ever to leave it because it felt so much like I'd finally come home.

Twenty-Six

When I woke again it was late the next day. I got myself into the bathtub, turned on the water and let it fill in around me. I stayed there a long time, because it felt safe. Finally the phone ringing got me up and out because it kept ringing. It wouldn't stop.

It was Beth. Her voice sounded tired and shaky, and she asked, "Where are you?" She said this like the pleading child I thought I'd become.

"What?" I asked, still confused it was her.

"Why aren't you here?"

The question seemed foolish, too foolish to answer but hanging up would only start the ringing again and that would hurt my head. It seemed best to try and wade through this now, so I said, "I didn't think you'd want to see me anymore."

She didn't say anything to this, not right off. When she did, she said, "Look, I'm coming over." And then she hung up.

I was sitting on the bed now still dripping wet. I curled up under the covers and stayed there damp and shivery.

In not so much longer I heard her knocking, a tentative sound I could almost ignore. But then it got like the ringing had, louder and more insistent until I could no longer pretend it away.

I got up and found a towel, pulled it around my waist, and opened the door.

She stood there fully dressed. She looked put together, and I wondered at my thinking she'd look like me—wet and disheveled and terribly in need. She came inside quickly, put her arms around me, and I heard her murmuring in my ear, over and over, "I'm sorry. Sweetheart, I'm so sorry."

I didn't know what I felt from this. I thought I should be the one apologizing. My body began to feel weak, even weaker, my knees giving in, my arms heavy around her. We went into the bedroom, or she took me there is really what happened. It started out like the night before—with me in the bed and her sitting beside me—except the feelings were all so completely reordered.

I felt nothing like anger, nothing close to it. In its place was a kind of fear and a stronger desire but not for where I knew we'd wind up. Still, that felt like the one way I could get close to what I needed—fucking her did. Or having her fuck me, but not like last night. Letting her have me her way.

She seemed in no hurry to get us there. She sat with me, calmly. Again just holding my hand. The bed began feeling soft and warm and maybe she felt warm, too, because she took off her coat first and then her shoes.

She curled up next to me. She still had her clothes on, and this left me feeling smaller somehow. To be the one already undressed, but then I found I liked feeling this way in relation to her. I felt something like trust.

She'd stopped saying she was sorry and I was glad for it because, more than anything else, that had confused me. That she believed she'd wronged me, didn't see it the other way around. I felt unsettled in a way I still couldn't shake.

Little bits of it lingered, making me inch when she touched me. Making me want to get up and get a drink or a cigarette. Making me want to do these things except for being the naked one, and this still feeling good but also leaving me someway trapped. And her having so much control again? It worried me. I couldn't stop it from worrying me.

But then she stopped it. Her hands on me did. Soothing and steady, they were smoothing me out. Pulling me under something as dark as an ocean. Something resembling that black sleep I'd just found, and so I went to it ardently. Went to her. Let her take me under.

She'd put her hands on my shoulders. She was pushing me back, and in this way I realized I'd stayed taut. Parts of my body had, bearing no resemblance to all the swimming softness inside me. She got under the covers with me, still in her clothes. I nestled against her. I wanted to undress her but this seemed beyond me, her clothes too intricate. I guess what I wanted was her undressed.

She just kept holding on to me, stroking me. I did finally manage to unbutton her blouse because her staying this way, her doing what I somewhere most wanted, I still couldn't allow it. It still made me need to do something else. I unfastened her bra, but once I had, I didn't go any further and so finally she was the one who took off her clothes.

Once she'd done this and we were still simply lying there, in the same way with no direction, she began saying things. The things I'd heard in my head the night before. I'd heard them so clearly then. But despite my wanting to, I could only half hear them now. Bits and pieces, reaching into me before fading. Then coming at me again.

This happening over and over, until I found them, somewhere, taking hold. And, for the first time, I saw all the questions inside these words. Could see how badly they needed answers. How badly she did. How much she needed me to answer the things she said with things of my own.

I didn't know how to do this without going back to last night. I knew she didn't want to and I didn't either, but I couldn't see another way. I said, "Ingrid's not who you think she is."

And I felt Beth immediately pull back from my having uttered this name, so I pressed on quickly. "To me, I mean. She's not who you've made her out to be. Can't you see this? And you're not who I thought you were either."

And I'd said this badly, too. Struggling on, I said, "That wasn't you last night, that was me. That's who I've always been. Can you understand I know this now? Can you understand I don't know who I am when I'm with you? When we're together? That you're no one I've known? Do you know what this means? What this means you mean?"

I'd become bogged down in my own swampy earth. Unable to explain something I'd only just happened on to. Unable to understand it myself, and now asking her to.

But, however ineptly, I must've given her some piece she needed. She came back to me in her comforting way. Hushing me. Saying, "Shush, shush now, sweetheart. I do know. I've always known. It's all right, now. Just be still."

She began to kiss me instead of just holding me and I kissed her back. And things began to dissolve then—my thoughts did, the stiffness left in my body. And with everything about me more fluid it was so much easier to become absorbed in her—my body going first and then taking my mind there. My feelings seemed to have been there all along.

She was partway on top of me, but I couldn't feel her weight. I had to shift in order to, and by doing this I realized she'd been

(192)

holding off me. In this physical way, she protected me. Everything about her tonight seemed to treat me as fragile. And my typical aversion to this gave way to its sweetness, to a larger thing of being cared for. Of letting her care for me. Believing she cared for me.

I didn't want to think anymore about the why of this. I didn't want to be brought back again to the night before, or to anything before. I wanted us to start over. To begin here and for it to change us, to change me.

I still believed the way to this was through my body and hers. I shifted again. Slid fully underneath her and then I could feel her weight. The whole of her giving in and pressing me down. And her lips pressing me too, first at my neck and my cheek—this way until I turned my head a little and opened my mouth. And when she put her tongue inside, I opened more.

The way she kissed me put me somewhere I couldn't recognize. It was too familiar. Familiar as something I'd wanted forever but never quite had. My arms were holding on to her. First around her back, but then I moved a hand to her neck, and then my other hand. I held her so gently.

She held fast to me, turning so I was beside her and then I'd wrapped around her. My legs first, then my arms. And she was wrapped around me, and this felt all at once rare and too close. I pulled away enough to kiss her neck and then her shoulders, and now she loosened and fell back. Lay before me in such a way it made me unable to move.

I don't know what I must've looked like, but what she saw made her move toward me in this hurried, comforting way. She began murmuring and it quieted me. Murmured more in sounds than words, and her hand went inside me with the same lilt as her voice. She seemed to know this always would soothe me.

And it eased me more this time than the others. For a while it made me feel wholly all right. And with this, too, the familiarity was one of wanting but never having.

She was so near to me but not so close I couldn't look at her and I did look. Maybe this was what made me go shaky again, the look on her face, which was both sad and gentle. Like she was still keeping herself back, keeping the things inside her away from me.

Her carefulness, I couldn't fathom it and so I closed my eyes. And when I did, I felt some last part of me giving to her. And now that I couldn't see her I could feel so much more of the things she felt. And maybe she knew this because she seemed even more to be staying away from me. Was still straining to stay off me and so I pulled her closer, wanting to be in that place where I couldn't tell us apart.

Her other arm came around my shoulders and she kissed me again. And I let her. I guess I'd always done this. She'd become one of the people allowed to have whatever they wanted of me. Do whatever they wanted to me. Maybe she was the only one left like that.

She began kissing my breasts and then sucking them. She lured me further and further under. And her hand stayed inside me that same soft way until a fullness came into my chest, but of a different sort than I'd let myself know before, even with her. Something very old and tired roved around in there.

I didn't try to stop it. Not then, and not when her mouth moved lower. First to my belly, and then nearer her hand. And I went lower, too. Deeper into myself when she let her hand come out of me, leaving only her mouth. I turned a little, and she helped my leg curl around her. She slipped just her finger into my ass and then what I recognized became beastly—wildly howling and ancient.

I don't think I made these sounds. They stayed lodged inside me, echoing there by themselves, alone, and so I felt alone or began to. Or maybe it went the other way around and the loneliness began this, tapped this place. A place so far inside me she couldn't get there, could only get me there. And now that I was—was there and alone—I most wanted her near me.

I knew she'd brought me here before. Taken me in this way, to this place. And that each time the same need was there—the one to crawl away. Each time exactly the same and not quite. Altering me by degrees. And this time that blackness, that dark sleepy thing besetting me. A sleep able to dampen that big baying mass, but somehow the same as it. Or the back of it.

This time I was trying to crawl away from me but not her. And when I couldn't, I tried to pull her in here with me, but I couldn't find my hands. I didn't know where they were.

I woke to them holding her hips. Woke because for a time I wasn't awake. Not asleep but not conscious either—in someplace where only my breathing mattered. Someplace between the baying and blackness. Suspended between them in half-light. And from here I could feel her but I didn't quite feel myself and so I couldn't know what had happened, not then, not fully.

I woke up to her stroking me, to coming in this huge, quiet way that made me want to cry except with all her carefulness, crying seemed too messy. This nearly put me back to sleep but instead I felt this other thing too, habitual, all about touching her, giving her something back.

I felt unable, though. Completely unable. She seemed content with this. Content with having had me and that I knew it this time.

If she left I didn't remember it. I did wake up alone, though. Alone and afraid and wanting her.

At least I began with wanting her until I remembered where she'd taken me. Remembered that leviathan thing I'd met inside me. That baying thing she'd let up and that black sleepy thing opposite. And, worst, that lost space between them. I could remember going there, being there, but had no memory of what happened outside it.

The fear of this led me to do something I knew not to. Something I knew should scare me, too. And, in any case, wouldn't work. Not the way I wanted it to, not anymore.

I called Ingrid. I tried to. I got her husband instead and so, of course, I hung up. Hung up wondering if he'd know anyway. Wondering somewhere in me always how much he knew, and why was he waiting because it felt that way all the time. Not that he'd let off me but was biding his time.

I wasn't at all clear what to do. I wound up getting dressed, taking some money from the envelope. Then I went to the store. Not the actual grocery store, which was way too far away, but a deli across the street. I bought food, though I wasn't hungry. I did better at the drugstore next door, bought things I might actually someday use. Then I went back home.

I soaked for a long time in the bathtub. Did this until something woke in me, telling me to get up and dressed because otherwise the phone might start ringing. That I needed to prevent this.

I went to Beth's office. I was late, I suppose. My sense of time so jangled by now, close was the best I could hope for. I saw her car there, parked where it always was. I nearly stopped, or did for a little bit, just to stare at it. I wondered how she kept up her life. How she kept it going normally through all of this. And so I went inside feeling suspicious of her in some way. Feeling away from her, that we weren't in sync.

She came to get me before I'd crossed the waiting room. She didn't touch me, but still there was this shepherding feel to the way she walked with me—a little behind, between me and the door, guiding and preventing escape.

I sat down right away, which left her the one standing. She stayed standing for a bit, close to me, then moving back toward her chair, stopping briefly to look at something on her desk.

I waited for her. And then we sat there looking at each other and saying nothing. She appeared a bit off, and tired too. Tired like me. This was reassuring, though I still wasn't sure whether she'd pretend last night away. And this time, I wasn't sure I didn't want her to pretend it away. Didn't need her to.

Maybe that's why I'd come here instead of letting her come to me. Maybe I thought it'd make all that go away. But she wasn't going to let that happen anymore. Already she held her hands out to me and I took them and then we were standing.

At first it felt like a long time ago, and safer because of this. But then I kissed her, awkwardly, like I didn't know what I was doing, and so already I'd given over to her. Given in to us being the same to each other day-to-day. The thing I'd thought I'd most wanted but now wasn't sure of.

She pulled at my shirt and put her hand underneath it and I began shuddering. I couldn't stop the shake in my legs, in one leg especially.

She seemed to be fighting something herself—her hands trembling and uncertain, staying for a long time with my breasts. She didn't really feel there. She didn't feel sure to me until she began touching my stomach, unbuttoning my pants.

I felt the need to move on her, to gain some kind of footing. But by the time this even registered she'd already gotten into my pants.

And then I was sinking to my knees and she with me. Her hand already inside me and the rest of her holding me up, and so here again she had me.

And, like last night, just when I thought I could let this be, let her have me, I couldn't. I wanted away. Away from that big baying thing coming up now to breathe. And I couldn't get away and I couldn't get my breath. It took all the air. And did she feel any of this in me?

Afterward, I couldn't go home. Instead, I went to the only other place that felt familiar—the parking lot. There weren't many people there and I had no clue about the trains. I'd lost track of the timetable. It'd been that long.

For these reasons I went into the bar, though as soon as I saw Burt and Jeremy, sitting at that same table, I realized they were why I had come.

I sat down without them asking me to. They barely noticed me, didn't say anything to me. They didn't miss a word in the conversation they were having, which seemed encoded. But then ordinary words gave me a lot of trouble these days.

When the waitress came over Burt ordered another round and tacked on a drink for me. A vodka, so at least he remembered something about me. I began to remember things about him. About them. I knew already this wouldn't work. And from here the urge to go home took me over. I felt too tired to walk, though. And even with money in my pocket and cabs waiting right outside, this way out didn't occur to me.

When I'd left off expecting him to, Burt turned my way. "Where've you been?" he asked.

But then he laughed like he already knew, and Jeremy laughed with him, and then he said to Burt, "I told you she'd turn up again. I told you we wouldn't need to make any effort."

I sat there, still not speaking or understanding. Sat there still with this tremendous urge to go home until I finally said it. Asked them would they take me there.

They both were laughing again and then we were all getting up and Burt was paying the bill.

Out in the parking lot, I found myself looking for that hapless guy. Expected to see him parked there and waiting. But I knew he wasn't, knew I would've noticed him on my way in.

I followed them across the lot to a nondescript car. Jeremy got in to drive. Burt motioned me in beside him, put his briefcase on the floor and pulled me into his lap. Once we got to my place he got out with me. He told Jeremy, "Why don't you go take care of that thing we discussed. This won't take too long." And then, like an afterthought, he said, "Give me the case."

He followed me up the stairs and into my apartment and then into the bedroom. He put the briefcase down and sat in a chair—one I'd almost forgotten because it was buried beneath clothes, clothes now strewn on the floor, except for a slip I'd also forgotten. Burt held this in his hands.

"Why don't you put it on," he said, and I hesitated for a few moments before taking it from him.

"I really need another drink," I said. "Do you want one?" I said these things as I made my way toward the door. He caught me by the arm and twisted. He said, "I've got something you want more." And I knew he meant drugs—even before he'd gone into his pocket, I knew.

He tossed two bags onto the bed. "Fetch," he said. Said it in such an ordinary way that I simply complied. When I started for them, though, he said, "Put that on first."

I took off my clothes, except for my underwear, started to pull the slip on over them but he told me to take them off.

"I don't think you'll be needing those, now will you?" This was what he actually said.

I couldn't decide what it was about him tonight that made me unable to disagree, made the things he said make sense. I didn't know whether it was anything about him really, or something about me. Where Beth had left me, what she'd left me with.

I clearly understood I'd gotten in over my head. I literally felt this way—underwater, my movements all slow and slurred. I crawled on to the bed, picked up the bag that looked more promising—full of pills I mostly recognized and a packet I knew held the thing I most wanted. The thing I'd needed badly since last seeing Beth, probably ever since I'd met her.

Her name crossing my mind again bothered me and not too long after I heard the phone. Heard it as I opened the packet and tapped some onto my hand and snorted.

Burt answered the phone. "She's busy just now." And then he unplugged the phone.

"Who was that?" I asked, as if he'd know.

"Just one of your girlfriends."

I snorted some more and this put me further underneath. Put me to a place I could keep going with this.

Burt took the other bag, the one full of coke, and he snorted some and he watched me, except I wasn't doing anything.

I was sitting on the edge of the bed, facing him. He told me to pull up the slip. I did what he said and then I opened my legs and he told me to touch myself. He said, "Come on, now, sweetheart. I want to see you."

I began this because it wasn't so foreign to me. He sat back and watched for a while before he held out the bag. And when I didn't move in response, he licked his finger and stuck it into the bag. Brought it out all covered in white and then he touched me, started with his finger almost inside me, running it along and in between.

I didn't feel much. Or at least what I felt seemed to come from his finger and not the drug, felt ordinary that way. I didn't feel enough off the heroin either, believed it should've kicked me down further given how long it'd been since I'd had any. But maybe because I'd spent so many months drowning, this couldn't compare. Couldn't take me any further down than Beth already had.

I found this acutely unsettling. I'd looked at this drug as something to count on. A last and sure thing that would hold her at bay and let me keep going. Something to keep my own baying in hand, make it heel.

I went into the packet again, took a lot more into my body, until I should've been sick but wasn't. Not in the physical way I expected. And this, the futility of it, made me want to be away from him, and from all of it. Be away from my life.

Nonetheless, I went through the motions. Did the things he told me to, which were no worse than things I'd done before. They only felt worse for the things in my head, going on in concert. These things being all about Beth, or the things in me she'd uncovered. No matter what I did, or what he did, I couldn't get rid of her, couldn't get rid of me.

That he wouldn't fuck me enraged me. And then I realized it wasn't about wouldn't, it was more about couldn't, and I became reckless and insulting. Felt power in this, in taunting him, until he pulled that briefcase onto his lap and opened it.

I couldn't see inside it and so when the gun came out, it startled me, though I don't guess it should have. What startled me more was him handing it to me. He said, "You want it so bad? Use this."

And when I didn't do anything, when I let the gun just hang limp in my hand, he yelled at me, "Do it." And then softer he said, "You'll do each thing I tell you."

I stared at the gun. It was heavy and looked old-fashioned. It had a long, dull-gray barrel, and the wood of the handle felt smooth and worn like he'd fondled it for years.

I still held it awkwardly, with my hand wrapped around it, around the trigger guard and the wood. The weight of it dragged my arm down, then started it shaking until I trembled all over.

"Cock it," he said.

It took some effort to pull back the hammer. I had to use both my hands to accomplish this. Had to rest my arms in my lap to steady them some. And while my body kept up this terrible shaking, my mind stayed completely still.

"Go on, fuck yourself," he said.

And here too I was slow and my dawdling got him yelling again. "Go on," he said first, and then the soft voice again. "You wanted it bad, right? Well, sweetheart, here you have it."

I put the barrel between my legs. I put my feet up on the bed and held myself open, and the rest of me upright. I slid it back and forth between my legs, felt everything go slippery there and in my head.

"Put it inside."

I did this easily, though the sighting notch caught me up a little, tore at me some.

"You like it?" he asked, but it wasn't a question. "You like it," he said, again.

I moved the barrel in farther and then out some. I found myself moving my hips in a way that sickened me, though the shaking had passed, taken over by arousal and nausea.

"Pull the trigger," he said. And I didn't feel fear or even anything like it. I didn't even pause. I just squeezed the trigger and felt myself squeeze round the barrel, and then I heard a cold click and the sound of his laughter.

I curled onto my side and curled up, still with the gun there inside me. He came over and opened my legs, which was not so easy to do. He took the gun back. Pulled a shirt from the floor and wiped the barrel off, still laughing but quieter.

I lay there and watched him, watched him flick the chamber open. Tip bullets into his hand—just two of them, clinking dully together.

He put the gun into his briefcase, the bullets into his pocket. And he plugged the phone in, had a curt conversation with Jeremy, and then he was gone.

This left me alone—alone with the packet. It didn't have much left in it. I searched around for a needle, already knowing I didn't have one. Still I went through everything. Looked in every drawer and every pocket with insatiable need. I kept searching and searching despite knowing I'd never find what just wasn't there.

Finally I gave up and went to bed, saving that last bit of junk because I figured I'd need it later. That it might not be so easy to get more. Or that what I'd have to go through to get it would take some days to face. This was what my life looked like now, looked like to me—just resting up for more of the same kind of thing that took me nowhere good.

I did rest. But I slept in that nodding, incomplete way. I'd expected this to feel comforting. The way it had when I was a kid, using that stuff in the beginning and it working so well. But it wasn't working now and I knew it had nothing to do with the method of delivery. I knew none of this old stuff would help me now. That Beth had opened someplace in me I might never get closed.

So I went to her office the next day, still addled and jangled. Sloppy from the rest of the dope, different but not different enough. Enough that she noticed, though. That when I went into her office and sat down, she took one look at me and said, "What's with you?"

And I said, "Huh?"

"You look like hell."

These statements were so plain, so direct, which still seemed so unlike her.

I said nothing in return. I just sat there because I seemed to have no idea what I was doing, where anything was going. Only had this horrible want to be in her bed and not mine. Strong enough I said, "Take me home with you."

It came out in that same reckless way, like the things I'd said to Burt. She looked startled. Like she was calculating things in her head. Things I couldn't know like the whereabouts of her husband.

Finally she said, "All right."

I felt a crazed glee. This fantastic belief everything would be okay now or at least better. I knew it showed. I knew I was smiling, and I could tell it concerned her.

We drove in silence pretty much. Once in a while she patted my thigh the way a mother might when something's not right.

We got to her house and once inside I went up the stairs. I'd taken my clothes off and gotten into her bed before she'd gotten into the room. She stood in the doorway for a bit. I couldn't look at her, turned my head away. I said, "Come here. I need you."

Hearing these words come out of my mouth unnerved me. Her, too, I'm sure from the way she sat beside me, still fully dressed and seeming unsure whether to touch me.

I touched her. I pulled her down beside me. Began kissing her, grabbing at her clothes. First her shirt, then her skirt, unable to stay focused on one or the other until I'd begun kissing her breasts and then sucking them.

She gave in then. I felt it. I felt her body change. She lay back and let me, and I was surprised at my energy. Didn't know where it could've come from, all in this sudden way that made me feel stronger.

I didn't take off her skirt, I just pushed it up; pulled her underwear aside and pressed into her. She tensed a little, and so I was the one telling her to take it easy. But then I stopped being easy myself, or maybe never had started.

I drove my hand into her. I wasn't sure what kind her cries were, not at first. I was afraid I was hurting her except it was clear I wasn't.

I didn't remember this, doing this before, seeing her this way. And her saying my name over and over—my real name. She hadn't done this before. Or, if she had, I hadn't let myself hear it. But that didn't matter, not exactly. Except that it did. It mattered most of all.

But now she'd left off this and was just making sounds, sounds I could get lost in. I watched her face intently. Watched her while she was coming. And when she'd finished she looked shy and defenseless as she curled into my body.

I had this sense of gathering her up. I pulled her as close as I could and this did feel better—having things the other way around. Somehow, through this, I felt all right. That we were all right—the two of us together. That we were together.

Feeling this way lasted a long while. Lasted until she shifted a little, was shifting me onto my back with her looking down on me. I wanted to change it again, change it back the other way, but something in her eyes kept me from trying, made me close my eyes instead.

I felt her body pressing the whole of mine, felt her hands along my sides, her thigh between my legs. And I was glad when she kissed me because I'd had the uneasy sense she was smiling, smiling out of wanting me, and I didn't like it.

I knew what she'd do before she started. Before she began to move her mouth down my body. And I knew her doing this would get me lost again. That she'd take me back to that place I loathed and craved.

I didn't bother anymore with trying to stop it. I just let it happen. And either the drug wasn't there anymore or it wasn't enough. That big wailing thing had taken up the whole of my chest and seemed to go further. I could feel it right through to my back, hurting me there. And I could feel it when she put her hand in me; I could feel it there, too. And I feared I couldn't keep the noises inside. That this sound echoing up into my mind was bigger than me.

But when the tears started, they weren't big. They trailed my cheeks slowly. I turned my face into the pillow to hide them, but it didn't work. I couldn't seem to hide anything. The whole of me, all my insides, mingled with what she was doing and I wasn't used to this overlap.

I began to make sounds. And they were about coming, but weren't only that. They were filled with that howling thing too, and unmistakably. So much so she nearly quit what she was doing until I told her, "Please …" And the sound of my voice was halting and haunting. I'd meant to say more but couldn't, not if it would sound this same way.

(206)

She finished me, then drew herself up beside me, and I clutched her and held on. She whispered these soothing things to me that weren't quite like words. She held me tightly. I didn't know which thing was breaking me, only knew I was broken.

And she knew too, but misplaced it. She'd seen I was torn, seen that tear from the gun. She said, "Sweetheart, what's happened? How'd this happen?" And her finger was there, fondling lightly, and so Burt was there too. And me trying to push him away but keep her. This made harder with them both calling me the same thing.

Her calling me that now, saying, "Sweetheart, tell me. Tell me who did this?"

Of course, I couldn't. So I tried to go back to the way I would've handled this before. I said, "Just some trick getting nasty."

But my voice sounded wrong, still came from too far inside me. Letting her too far inside me. And letting that baying thing loose again. Letting it out where she might maybe see it. And maybe she had seen it, or sensed it, because she took her hand away from that tear and put it onto my chest. Began to fondle me there. Did this so slowly, and kept on that way even once my tears came again.

And she still stayed steady and slow when I couldn't keep hold of myself anymore. When that howling thing took me over. When it had me at bay, or she did. When she was laying down with it. Laying me down with it, in it. Until it was all of me, or she was.

Twenty-Seven

I spent the night with her. I nearly did. She woke me up before it was light out and this felt superstitious to me. That someway if we never woke up together in the morning, in the light, it kept this thing between us not quite real, or in some separate place.

She drove me home in the half-light of dawn and I thought, What will we do as the days get longer, how will we keep our meetings always at twilight? How will it change things? And so from this dead space that was still winter I asked, "Where's your husband?"

I surprised myself with this question and also with where it had come from. She looked stunned by it. I actually believed she was weighing the ethics of telling me her problems. That this slowed her answer. It seemed both ridiculous and sweet.

"He's moved out for a while. We needed some time apart."

She said this as if it had nothing to do with me and maybe it didn't. At least I could believe this. I wondered whether she could, or even was trying to.

Once I was home—in my own bed by myself—I couldn't believe it at all. I could only see I'd busted another marriage. To even imagine this felt dangerous. Like this hole in me getting bigger and more torn at the edges would just keep growing until it'd taken me over. And I could see it making holes in other people, in Beth. Tearing at her life as well.

I thought of calling Burt because, for the moment, drugs seemed the answer. That one drug did. Calling him wasn't possible though, not having his number or a clue to his last name. And this meant facing Beth again, with this new knowledge and nothing to bolster me.

I began drinking soon after. It didn't work very well. It only reminded me I needed so much more in order to cope. The one thing it did accomplish was to keep me at home. It placed me where I thought I should stay—in my bathtub, surrounded by warm water and with a glass propped on the edge of the tub, the bottle on the floor beside me.

I'd even brought the phone in and doing this reminded me Beth had said nothing about talking to Burt. And nearly on cue the phone rang and I felt afraid to answer it.

I let it ring a long time and when I picked it up different voices sloshed around in my head. Made the voice actually there hard to make out.

"Nina? Nina, he knows you called. I've been phoning for two days but you never answer."

"Ingrid," I said as some sort of horror crept in beside, or through, all the booze.

"Listen to me, now. It's not safe anymore."

"Did you call last night?" I asked, then realizing I had the day wrong.

"I've been calling. Have you been there?"

"What?"

"Who was that? That man? I thought I knew him. I know his voice."

Gradually I understood she'd been the one to call that other night. And instead of concerning me, this saddened me—that it hadn't been Beth after all. I sat there thinking, Well maybe she called later. I puzzled this while Ingrid kept saying, "Nina. Nina, it's important you listen to me now."

I didn't really listen. I couldn't. Though some part of me had gone into motion. I was getting out of the tub. Knocked the glass on the floor, then picked it up. I carried it, and the bottle and the phone and a robe, into the living room because the bedroom seemed too dark and ugly.

I sat on the couch and tried very hard to grasp what she was saying. But all I kept hearing was that name I'd given her to call me, her saying it over and over. And then I stopped struggling to hear anything else because what could I do? And once I stopped trying, I began understanding her, accomplishing this all too well.

"Nina, he might come for you. I don't know what he'll do."

"He doesn't know where I am."

She was slow to say anything to this. And I knew he could've found me without her. This didn't trouble me, even him coming after me didn't. What troubled me was knowing she'd given him the map.

I realized this wasn't new knowledge, so it hurting so much surprised me. The wrong things always seemed to be hurting me. Stealing too much of my attention so I could never focus on protection.

Finally she said, "Nina, if he wants to he'll find you."

And with you there to help him—this was what I felt like saying but what actually came from my mouth turned me full circle. I said, "I want to see you. Ingrid, I need to see you."

"Darling, that's the worst thing we could do."

"I could come there," I said. "He wouldn't expect that."

I didn't know why I was saying these things. I didn't know where they were coming from except that maybe these days nothing could scare me more than the things Beth gave rise to. And if those things lived inside me all the time anyway, how could anything else ever actually hurt me?

"It's too dangerous," she said flatly. "It'd only make things so much worse."

"But ..." I started and then trailed off. I knew I'd likely never see her again. That if I was too dumb or desperate to protect myself she didn't share this. She'd protect herself. She'd always been better at that than me.

I pulled the robe closer around me. I said, "Don't worry. I know you're right." Then, without saying anything more, without saying goodbye, I hung up.

The phone didn't ring again and I didn't know why I wanted it to. I went into the bedroom, into the drawer with her money. There was still plenty there, enough maybe even to leave, except I knew I wouldn't do this.

What I did instead was get dressed. If I left soon, I could go by the bar before I saw Beth. I did this but I didn't find Burt and Jeremy. I settled for buying a bag off a guy at the bar and smoking it there in the bathroom. I thought this might get me further than snorting. It didn't. Not very. Though it did get me to Beth's. Late again and not exactly well put together.

I tried to remember where she and I had last been. Could only remember her driving me home. Now that I was with her I couldn't place what had come before. But somewhere I must've known because I couldn't sit down for the longest time. It'd been quite a while since I'd felt the true need for this game. It had become only a habit.

When I finally sat down and looked at her, what I saw was genuine concern and a tenderness that made me want to spill out all the things going on inside and around me. Make use of her the way I should've all along. But my skills for taking care of myself were so misaligned I stayed wary.

What occurred to me instead was trying to use her place to hide. That if I could keep spending my nights there he might not find me so easily.

Something about her made this seem impossible. I couldn't quite discern what it was. The drug emboldened me enough to ignore it. But it wasn't doing much of anything else. And even though I knew this wasn't about the way I'd put it into my body, that didn't mean I wouldn't go back to get more.

I waited for her, waited for her to say anything. She looked tired in a way that made me wonder if she'd really spent the day here working. Or if like me she'd spent the day somewhere else and had only recently arrived.

I kept looking for a way in—a way to ask could we go to her place. Not finding it made me think beyond her reasons, and clear through to my own. I couldn't drag her into this. I couldn't put her at risk because what if he found me there? This led to the new problem of then where would we go? I sure couldn't take her to my place, and I couldn't tell her why, and staying here seemed too uncomfortable.

I muddled this over while she continued not to speak. I got so lost inside my own skull that when she did finally say something I didn't hear her. I didn't even know she'd leaned toward me. Not until she was jostling my knee. And then I noticed how close our chairs were again. I stayed with this thought, wondering when she'd moved them. Then she took my hand and said, "Hey, are you there? Are you there at all?"

"Huh," I said, which I'm sure sounded convincing.

"Are you on something?"

I thought this a ridiculous question. She hadn't exactly worried about this yesterday. Yesterday, she'd liked me on junk. She'd liked the way I'd fucked her.

I pulled my hand away from hers and crossed my arms against my chest. I said, "Sweetheart, I'm always on something. Hell, you like it that way."

She pulled back, too. She looked stung and disappointed and I was disappointed, too—in myself and this childish game I still couldn't let go of.

She was staring out the window, though not really since the shade was drawn. As if without meaning to, I'd gotten up. Not to get away from her, but to go to her. I was kneeling in front of her. I'd taken her hand. "I'm sorry," I was saying. "I didn't mean that."

My other hand was on her thigh, first over her skirt and then slipping underneath it. I was stroking her, pushing her skirt up a little.

I slid my hand between her legs, trying very hard to keep as gentle as she would've. She still wasn't looking at me and so I stopped looking at her. I pushed her skirt up farther and undid just the one stocking. Pulled it a little ways down and began kissing her thigh. I felt better about this when she put her hands in my hair. When she leaned back and let go some, opened her legs more.

I took off her underwear. Put my arms around her and pulled her closer. Began to kiss her and lick her until she started making sounds. And from this, I stopped worrying.

When I'd finished her, I stayed on my knees and held on. She didn't move. She stayed quiet and kept her legs wrapped around me. This felt comforting before it began feeling that same too-close way. But then she took my hands and pulled me onto her lap, facing her. Now it seemed she knew more of what happened inside me than I did, or could ever.

She held my face in her hands. Looked at me in a way I didn't know. Saw me as someone I didn't know. I stayed with her eyes before I closed mine. Did this when she kissed me, first near her hands and then on my throat. Finally kissing my mouth and me opening mine, tipping my head back into her hands, feeling them stroking my neck, one of them opening my shirt.

My body went taut before it went loose, and then she was trying to get up. At first I didn't know what it meant. She was saying, "Come on, sweetheart."

She'd taken my hand, was leading me out of there and into the waiting room, to that big wide couch where I lay down.

She lay down beside me and was stroking my chest. She let the whole of her hand rest between my breasts, staying there long enough that all those same feelings settled underneath it. I took a breath that spread me out. It left me shaking and needing way too much.

She'd unbuttoned the rest of my shirt. Had begun on my pants. She did all this so slowly. It seemed wherever her hand went it found more of my need. And then she followed her hand with her mouth, and nothing had felt so soft to me as that couch. It took in my body and so I lay there, letting my breaths come in this deep, faltering way that made me afraid of what else they'd uncover.

I wanted to touch her but couldn't move my arms. I just let them lay there beside me while she did these things to me. While she kept stroking me, my stomach, and then between my legs—

stroking me in this soothing, soft way that left me dumbstruck. And when her fingers went into me they stayed soft and didn't stay long and then went back inside me. I knew I'd never known this before, not in this way. That if I could've asked, could've spoken at all, it would've been to make her stop this.

My breaths were halting and turning into sobs and I didn't want her to see this. I didn't want her to know this about me except she already did. She knew more what I'd needed always than I did.

I didn't try to stop any of it any longer. Instead I let myself wail and bawl and, when I tried to curl up, she put her weight on me. Kept me still so I couldn't. Brought me off in that way I couldn't distinguish from the rest of it. That way that was part of the rest of it. Or only that, that howling massive mess.

And then she'd put her hand so deep in me, drew the rest of her body up next to me, close to me, and I felt my hands holding her hand in me. Felt my legs fall open while I held her hand inside me, and she just kept saying, "It's all right, sweetheart. It's all right now."

She said this again and again until I believed it. Then I let go of her hand and grabbed hold of her, pulled her to me. I wrapped my legs around her and this put me back to that howling place, but she kept talking to me, and I could hear her. I could hear her there with me.

She kept telling me it was all right. She said this with such unmistakable love, and I loved her, too. I loved her so much in that moment, it seemed nothing, no one, could hurt me again. Like this feeling for her bathed that hulking place that'd been so sore, sore from my very beginnings.

The trouble was how to ever get up from this. It seemed Beth would stay with me as long as I needed, and longer. That I'd have to be the one to end this.

As it grew light out I worried the things I thought ought to worry her, like what if the other people who worked here began coming in to start on the day.

But this didn't trouble her and so I realized I'd lost all sense of days and weeks. Understood it must be a weekend. I couldn't otherwise account for her ease.

I dipped in and out of sleep, but each time I woke she was still there awake and with her arms around me—us curled up together and her sometimes stroking my hair.

All this endless patience in her tested mine. Asked, Did I want to stay or go? And it left me trying to determine what else I could possibly want from her because it seemed there was something else. Someway even this wasn't enough and never could be.

I sank back into her arms, back into sleep because I thought that there maybe I wouldn't have to know this anymore. Wouldn't have to know that everything left me still wanting. And that this want seemed to stretch on forever and roll backward too. It mingled with a need that came before and ahead of everything else and would keep on with me, endless and relentless and never served.

I did sleep, but it wasn't the deep kind. Not the black, empty kind I wanted. I kept waking and then dozing. Pretended sleep when I could no longer achieve it for real. And by then what I hoped for was her sleep. That she'd drop off and let me steal away.

She didn't do this, though. And she showed no sign that she would. Instead she kept steady, kept watch over me in this same tender way until restlessness took hold in my limbs.

I wondered if loving her would accomplish what I needed, so I began this in a halfhearted way. Turned into her because she'd settled behind me. I began to kiss her softly but she took this easy. Took it the way she'd taken everything for so many hours.

She quieted me. She said, "Sweetheart, just rest." And the words changed me from restless to sad; not huge and crazed now, but quiet and ageless. Her ease took me over, and my tears in her shirt—all of her wrapped around me. I cried easily this time, hushed and tranquil and endless.

Twenty-Eight

When I did finally leave, she didn't drive me. I went by myself. And walking home in that late afternoon, I felt changed. Even knowing it wouldn't last. That I could barely keep hold of it now. That with each step I took, it went further from me. Or stayed with her. Still, I believed some small piece would remain, maybe show me the way out.

At the same time I knew this was far off for me and I might never get there. Might not get through the things coming before. I could see it but was nowhere close to it.

I went into my apartment this way. Took a bath, went to bed and slept. Slept that black way I craved. And I woke the next day, which was Sunday, still some small way different. It wasn't the presence of something so much as the absence. The things pressing me so hard had given way just a little.

I stayed in bed. I lounged there half sleeping. And when I heard a knock at the door, I went to answer it in just my T-shirt and underwear—that's how certain I was I'd find Beth.

They came in all together in a rush. Jeremy grabbed hold of me. For a moment my body stayed heavy—deadweight in his arms before I began struggling. I heard his soft laugh in my ear, and his arms grew tighter and stronger, and then he had me face down on the bed.

I didn't raise my head. I didn't want to see anything. But he'd grabbed me by the hair, lifted my head this way until I had to lift it myself or feel more of this prickly kind of hurt.

Burt stood in front of me. He had that same gun in his hand and a smile on his face. He said, "You want something to suck on? You look like you could use something to suck on."

He put the gun far into my mouth until it scraped the back of my throat. My head grew groggy and heavy and so Jeremy was holding it up and the stinging from this worked to keep me awake. But I didn't want to be awake.

I felt Jeremy shift. He tucked his arm underneath me. Lifted me to my knees and I wobbled on the too-soft surface of the bed. His weight was behind me, pressing against me, and I leaned back into him to get my balance.

This made the gun slip a little and so Burt grabbed my hair. A big handful of it that started a duller pain, but it let Jeremy stop pulling on it.

Burt said, "Come on, sweetheart. Show me something. Show me what you do best."

I tried to. But it seemed I couldn't control my body well, any part of it. My mouth had gone all slack around the gun. I didn't like the taste of metal and the scraping. I kept trying to get away from these two things. Tried without trying. My mouth wouldn't hold on to it the way he wanted.

I had this want to explain. Tell him I would do what he said if only I was able. But I wasn't able to talk either.

He said, "Suck it, now, or I'll blow you."

What let me do this was Jeremy. He'd put his extra hand into my underwear, was playing with me and it gave me a strange safety. Something to feel besides already dead.

I found myself moving my hips back and forth against him. And then with him. I tunneled into this and sucked the gun. Moved my head back and forth with Burt helping me, him sliding the gun in and out of my mouth. Still lifting my head for me.

"That's right," he said. "That's it." And his voice sounded gentle now and the comfort I felt from this seemed wrong but no less soothing for it. And so that's how I felt—soothed but sickened, sickened at the way these two things so often arrived together.

This kept on and on. I'd closed my eyes because it made it easier to feel what Jeremy was doing. Let me keep what I was doing for Burt a little away. But, like he knew he didn't have my attention, Burt jammed the gun hard until it'd ripped all of my mouth. And then he yanked my hair so I was looking right up into his eyes.

He pulled the gun out and slid it along my cheek, then across my lips. Did this before he handed it back to Jeremy. My body went all soft again without Jeremy's hand and my arms ached suddenly and fiercely. I began sinking forward until Burt yanked me up again.

He'd undone his pants. "Come on now, sweetheart," he said, putting his dick in my mouth. It felt soft and small, like it couldn't hurt me the way the gun had. And Jeremy having the gun felt better until he began to slide it back and forth between my legs.

"You want Jeremy to fuck you? I think that's what she's been wanting."

Jeremy still just rubbed me with the gun for a little bit. My legs ached now, all of me ached. And I ached the way Burt meant, too, and so when Jeremy put the gun into me I didn't know what I wanted or where I was in myself. But all of it changed when he pulled it out again. When Burt said, "Fuck her ass." And then this sharp, tearing pain shoved me forward.

I would've cried out. Maybe I did, but Burt's dick was still there muffling everything except this pain that wouldn't quit. I kept waiting for it to. My body that'd been so slack now went the opposite. Tight in this way I couldn't undo, nothing in me able to stop that spiking barbed thing inside me.

Burt stood there, laughing a little. He said, "You're going to suck me off, sweetheart. You understand me?"

And his dick went half-hard from him saying this because I knew I hadn't accomplished it. And I knew what he wanted of me was impossible. That he couldn't get any harder than he already was, much less come off. And so I saw too clearly the beauty of my position.

"You understand?" he said again. "Because otherwise, Jeremy's pulling the trigger."

He yanked at my hair more. He said, "You like that, don't you, sweetheart? Knowing the chamber's full? Is that enough to satisfy you? Huh? Answer me."

He pulled at me harder, yelling this last thing again and again. And then he pulled at my hair some more, made it like I was nodding my head. And Jeremy pushed harder, too, pushed the barrel farther and farther so the hurt inside me never let up. And this horrible heaviness took hold in my chest. Dragged me toward the bed. Left the two of them pulling and pushing at me all the more, or making me feel it worse.

And when I thought it would keep on this way forever, Burt began laughing. Not quietly, but loud. Like the joke on me was even better than I'd thought. And then he was taking his dick away and zipping his pants and, when I'd sunk to my elbows, he leaned down and stroked my cheek. His laughter had turned to a low chuckle. I watched him walk out into the living room, saw him settle on the couch, with my phone in his hand. I watched him get on with his next piece of business.

Jeremy took the gun out of me, and while he did this slowly there was still the tearing and it made me jerk my head around and see for the first time the other one in the room. The guy from the car who'd done all that waiting in parking lots, and had waited through this, too. But before I could wonder what all his endless patience might mean for me, Jeremy took me back again. And so it was that much clearer they were nowhere near finished with me.

Jeremy laid the gun near my head. It stayed lifeless there, leaving this little streak of blood on the sheet. I felt lifeless, too. A short moment of sweetness in this before Jeremy pushed me down and then was pushing into me. Trying to get his dick into my ass. My body went from dead to too alive all in a quick rush of soreness. And unwilling or unable or both, I knew I couldn't take him. There just wasn't room in me for this.

He wouldn't stop trying though. Not for the longest time and by now I'd given in to just crying. This occurring somewhere inside me while on the outside I didn't feel any tears or cries or movement, just the limping, unmanaged jerks of my body. Of it reacting to things. I couldn't be sure if I felt anything at all.

And then maybe I wasn't wholly there for a time because what I felt next was the other man's arms around me. Him behind me and me leaning against him. I felt his hands in my T-shirt, heard him in my ear, saying in a voice I'd never heard, "You're going to like me. You'll see."

And I wondered whether I was alone with him until I opened my eyes and saw Jeremy still there, loafing on the bed. He still had the gun. Was fucking me with it in a way I could only watch. I had no other way to know it was happening.

My head lolled back against this other one, which seemed to please him. I felt the stubble of his beard scratching my cheek and his hands still fooling with my breasts. Of all of it, I seemed to have the most trouble with this.

I tried to rest. I felt so tired. I closed my eyes again but still it took me some time to get away. To stop feeling the one behind me, him fondling me.

I must have at some point managed it, though, because a slicing across my belly and an instant numbing there startled me back awake. I opened my eyes to see Jeremy lapping a little coke off my stomach. I could feel this little damp place left by his tongue. From the look of things, the look of me, he'd been doing this a while. All across my belly these little hash marks from his knife. This last one maybe just went deep enough to impress me. Went deep enough that the coke spilled into it, making this pinkish clump.

He noticed me. Licked a bit from his knife and then scooped more onto it. Held the knife to my face and told me to have some. "You need to wake up," he said.

I jerked my head away but the one behind me stopped that, held me still until I snorted some. Jeremy cleaned the blade on my cheek. Then he wiped it on my shirt, which they'd cut off me apparently. It lay near me in pieces.

Jeremy snorted lines off my belly, then smeared what was left into those little scratches. He closed his knife and instead of feeling glad for this I felt suddenly scared because he was getting up to leave, to go join Burt in the other room. This would leave me alone with the last one.

Jeremy closed the door most of the way when he left. I could hear him and Burt talking but I didn't think it was about me. This last guy came around from behind me and I fell back until first the bed and then the wall stopped me. My head hitting the wall woke me more than the coke had.

He was sitting on my chest. He had his hand behind my neck and was lifting my head toward his lap. He pressed my face against him for a while. Rubbed himself against me until I could feel him getting hard through the soft cloth of his pants.

He took his dick out and rubbed it along my face and the softness of this and his pants meant it hurt more when his zipper scratched my cheek.

This all seemed nearly friendly so when he began yelling, it caught me short. I didn't know what I'd done. Had trouble making out the things he was saying. They seemed to come from his throat all clumped together, and so I'd only get little bits until he screamed, "Open your fucking mouth."

Then his fingers were opening it for me, prying me open. And once he got his dick inside, he fucked my mouth hard enough that my head kept hitting the wall. I slid down to try and stop this. To stop the pounding back of my skull, not to get away from him. But my moving made him slip out.

Then he got rough. He pulled his belt from his pants and doubled it over, smacked me across the face. And I could hear the sound of this and him still shouting, shouting, "Oh, you'll do them, huh? And not me."

And it going on this way in a rant about me thinking him not good enough, and I was wanting to tell him that wasn't it at all. That I was just very tired. That if he'd let me rest, just for a while, I'd do whatever it was he wanted.

I was beyond speaking, though. Had lost this ability way before his belt pulped my lips.

He left off the smacking, finally. Looped the belt around my neck just as Ingrid's husband had. He tried to tie my hands with it, but his girth wasn't big enough and so the belt wasn't long enough and this angered him too. He yanked me up by it before he let go and got off the bed.

He sorted through all those clothes still in a heap on the floor. Came back with a belt from a robe, one Ingrid had borrowed while she was here. This cord was sure long enough, and made of a stretchy, scratchy synthetic that made his job easier and mine harder. Harder still when he hog-tied me with it.

I'd never been in exactly this position before. And when he turned me on my back I had to scramble for space in my throat—this cord clutching it and tightening and never seeming to give way no matter how I arranged myself.

I pulled my legs up under me, or my feet really. Kept them close together underneath me but my legs wide open before him. Held myself up with my thighs, the muscles in them waking up angry, forcing me to feel that part of my body again.

None of this worked. My wrists were down too close to my ankles and all the slack was in the wrong place. And this tugging around my neck wouldn't stop, didn't really stop even when I got my hands up under my shoulder blades. I kept trying to lift myself up, get myself off the cord. But I wasn't doing well at this, and he was pressing down on my legs, and then pressing them farther apart until I had to give way and wait him out.

I couldn't not feel how he fucked me. Felt it more for all the feeling that had come back to my legs. I felt everything—the cutting in my wrists and ankles, my throat closed off, and the only good thing about this was it kept me from crying out loud. This feeling like some kind of victory until I realized it served him for me to be quiet.

(225)

He kept pounding at me until I went numb despite all the things stacked against it, though maybe it was just my blood wasn't moving. That it couldn't get past the cord anymore.

When he pulled out, I tried to turn on my side, turn away, but he was over me again, jerking off on my chest and my face until finally he went away. I curled up inside-out of how I wanted to be. My arms and legs behind me instead of tucked up in front of me. I was retching and trying to spit but my throat stayed too raw. I turned my head into the sheets to wipe his come off me. I kept turning my head into the sheets.

And, too, I listened. Heard them all moving around and talking, all these bustling noises, which I wanted to mean they were leaving.

But before they did, they came back to me. Burt said, "Just one more thing, sweetheart." And I'd hated his calling me this all along, but hated it most now when I'd just begun to let myself think of Beth.

Burt said, "Gabriel wants a little trophy."

I saw Jeremy had his knife out. I began to scramble. This coming before I could think about Ingrid's husband having sent them—something I seemed to have known all along anyway.

"He wants proof we were here."

Even with me still tied, it took the three of them to hold me down. Jeremy ran his fingers through my bush, smoothed it before he pulled at it. Before Burt said, "I can see why he'd want that pelt." I began struggling again but only inside myself. I didn't want them taking this piece of me I'd only just realized I felt vain about.

He was still tugging on me, and then he rubbed at my clit. He said, "I think I want this for myself." And in me this turned-on terror, this frothy airy stuff working my chest and running inside my head, not letting me leave.

(226)

He laughed and then tugged at my bush again. He said, "Don't worry, darling. We won't take the one thing you need."

I didn't move when he cut. It seared, felt warm in this way, but maybe that was my blood. He was quick about this, businesslike. And when he'd done it, I fell away from them.

He cut the cord and, soon as I could, I curled up. Curled up as tight and small as I could and just lay there, not moving, not hearing, not crying, not registering anything. Except Burt saying one last thing, "Here's your souvenir. I figure you've earned it. Hell, sweetheart, I think you're going to need it one day soon." And he tossed a bullet my way. It thumped my back before falling somewhere behind me.

Twenty-Nine

When I woke from this stupor I knew they'd left. Still, I didn't move. I found I could move but didn't. I didn't want to look at what they'd done. I'd balled the sheets between my legs and could only see blood there.

When I finally untangled myself, it wasn't as bad as I'd thought. They'd taken a strip from the side, not the whole of it. Still, when I made it into the bathroom, into the bathtub, the water stung. The thing hadn't stopped bleeding and so the water was at first reddish and then turning less so as it filled in around me, becoming a lighter and fainter pink.

I stayed there until I felt scared again. Got out in a sudden rush that dumped water all over the floor. I found a towel lying in the sink. One they must've used because it had these swipes of brownish red. And when I saw this I dropped it, but then I picked it up again because I was shivering too much to move and find another.

I went into the bedroom, but in there were just more reminders and I needed badly to forget this. I stumbled around, bumped into things until I found my robe, and then the phone—this on the coffee table, near an ashtray and two glasses, a bottle of vodka they'd been into.

I got my own glass. Sat down on the couch and poured a drink. I stared at the phone. But I didn't pick it up until I felt the robe—thin terry cloth sticking to me. And then I saw the blood matted to it, still spreading through the weave. Saw that I still hadn't stopped bleeding.

I called Beth. She answered, sounding as sleepy and groggy as me, and I felt lonelier than I maybe ever had, her being there making me feel it more instead of less. I said, "I need to see you. I'm in real trouble."

Her voice got suddenly clear and awake. "Are you home? I'll come there."

And I looked around the room and through the bedroom door, and said, "No. I mean, I'm home but please don't come here."

"Sweetheart, what is it? What's happened?"

"Can I meet you somewhere?"

She took over then. She said, "Go to my office. I'm leaving right now."

But she held on the line until I hung up first.

Now I felt better for having things to do, though I couldn't do them well or fast. I tried putting on underwear but it hurt too much, catching that piece of me that wasn't there. And the first few pairs of pants I tried felt the same way—hurtful, nicking me if I moved. I searched the floor and then my drawers for the loosest softest clothes I could find.

I ended up with a baggy pair of army fatigues, worn thin and soft. Found a crumpled bit of foil in the pocket, which only served to remind me how long I'd lived this way. But it didn't stop me from hunching over it—half-naked with a lighter—trying to smoke what might be left in it.

I pulled an old shirt of my father's from a bottom drawer, the fabric so old you could see through it. From habit, I tried tucking it in, but this hurt too, so I just let it hang, buttoned it the best I could and then began growing worried about all the time this was taking.

I put shoes on, put Beth's coat on, finally found my keys and started for her office.

It was colder outside than I'd imagined and so I pulled the coat around me, feeling drafts everywhere through my loose clothes. I hadn't managed socks, so my ankles felt it worst. The wind ate into the burns from the cord.

I trudged along, watching headlights coming at me and wondering what I must look like. I'd stayed far away from mirrors, not wanting to know this.

I arrived before Beth did, and so I sat on the little concrete step outside the door there. My hands were jammed into the coat's pockets. I found a pack of cigarettes I'd left there and a lighter. I smoked one after another, my lips feeling too big, numb, leaving blood on each filter. I did this mechanically until her car turned in.

She came toward me, quickly crossing the lot, and seeing her, I felt suddenly dead. I stood beside her as she fumbled with her keys and the door. Caught a glimpse of her in the light there. Saw her seeing me and I didn't like how she looked.

Once she got us inside I shucked her coat on my way to the couch. Already I knew she couldn't give the fixing I needed.

I curled up on the couch with my back to her. Wanted her with me, and not. The sight of her had started these sobs in my chest, and then in my throat. Hurting me because of the rawness, how torn I was there. But I still couldn't stop. Couldn't stop from sobbing, though it seemed so important to, more this time than ever.

I felt her hand on me, on my shoulder, uncertain but still soft and so making my crying that much harder to control until I left off trying. And then she'd curled behind me and was holding on, and for a time this was helping.

We wound up turned around. She was propped against the couch's arm with me leaning back in her arms. Her hands were stroking me. It felt sweet, having her hands on me, until one of them went into my shirt, which I hadn't buttoned well, and this wildness started from her fondling me, my breasts.

This simple thing crippled me, made me unable to move and so I didn't, but went tight in her arms and this started her talking. Saying those things she always said, and her hands moving along my stomach and me feeling the little cuts there, but her seeming not to. All this continued until she got into my pants and I jerked away when she found the gash there.

The feel of it must've startled her too, because she yanked away the same moment I did. Then her arms were around me again, and there was blood on her fingers, and she kept saying, "What's happened to you?" and "Who did this?"

I lay there mute, letting her keep on this way until it'd run its course and then she was quiet, except for saying, "Oh, sweetheart," again and again. And her mouth was close to my ear and her kissing me near there, now and then.

I felt my body letting go, leaning heavy into her, deadly. Her arms felt heavy too. A solid weight, lulling me. I think maybe I even drifted off, or half did. I remember feeling so tired again. I didn't want ever to have to get up from this.

But then she was getting us up. Held me tight around the waist and walked me to her car. Came around my side and opened the door for me, helped me in. I didn't know where we were going. Panicked a minute she might turn toward the hospital or the police station. But she turned the other direction, which meant either my place, or hers.

I knew she'd take me home. Much as I didn't want to go back there, I couldn't tell her. I hadn't spoken at all this whole time we'd been together. I knew no matter how hard I wished it, we wouldn't be going to her place. That I wouldn't find myself in her bed, which seemed the only place I wanted to be, the only safety I could think of.

I knew my place was safe, too. In the real sense of it. I knew they were done with me, that Ingrid's husband was. That I'd never see any of them on purpose ever again. But going back there still felt very bad. And the closer we came, the further away went all that soothing and lulling until in its place were these bands wrapping my chest tighter and tighter. Wide but thin—sheet metal full of a strange current, filling me with a jagged, ragged energy that left me useless and disabled.

When we got there, Beth nearly had to pull me from the car. So much so, I heard her ask, "Is someone still there?" Heard her ask this in an unnerved way, like this had only just now occurred to her and she was frightened by it.

I shook my head in a disjointed motion that hurt my neck and I felt my hand go to my throat, felt the burns again, and it hurt inside too, it wouldn't stop hurting there.

She put her arms under mine and then around me when she'd got me to my feet. And then she walked me like you would an invalid. She walked me to the door and then through it and up the stairs. All the way, she was saying little things like, "It's not so very much farther."

When we got to the door she had to fish my pockets for the keys—that's how worthless I was. And her going into my pants stirred that sore and so I cried more, yelped even a little. And she said, "We're almost there, sweetheart. Almost there."

(232)

She put me on the couch and looked around the place. I took my glass, or someone's, from the table and sucked at the vodka while she tried to make some kind of order of things.

I felt embarrassed. Ashamed of how it looked, at how much you could tell by looking. She brought me a blanket and wrapped it around me. She let me keep my drink.

Through the door, I watched her changing the sheets. Felt more shamed by this than anything so far, and more cared for. These two things made me slump back, loosening those bands wrapping my chest until I found myself crying again—quietly at first and then heaving from it, afraid this time I'd never stop.

Then she'd come over to me. She put the bullet on the coffee table without a word about it. That stopped me crying. She led me toward the bedroom and I found myself that same way as in her car. Fighting her every step, and her being that same way too, saying, "It's all right now. No one's going to hurt you." But I no way believed her.

She got me in there and undressed me. There were pillows behind me and the sheets felt good, soft and clean, and this calmed me some until I remembered the last one to change them was Ingrid. This sent me taut again, and Beth had gone away, had gone into the bathroom. I found myself afraid they'd stolen the money, Ingrid's money. But Beth was back before I had time to check the drawer and know for sure.

She had a bowl of soapy water and some washcloths, a bottle of alcohol, all these things in her hands. She put them on the bedside table, started dabbing at me with one of the cloths, cleaning my face. I felt childlike. It stung when she got at my face with the alcohol, when she bathed my neck with it. And so I behaved like a child, quivering when she put her fingers to my lips, mewling when they came back bloody.

I didn't want her to see the rest of me. I'd pulled the covers up and wouldn't let them go. She pried at my fingers. Told me, "Just lie down, now. Sweetheart, let me do this."

I gave way to her. She seemed so much stronger than me, and this made me see I'd always thought I was the strong one of the two of us. I started to wonder if maybe this notion was as wrongheaded as the rest of my thinking.

The cloth on my wrists made them feel better, but when she got to my stomach it hurt again. Stung from the touch of it, and then more when she used the alcohol.

I didn't want her to tackle that real cut. I wanted her to leave it alone, but I knew she wouldn't. Getting to it stopped her, though. Caught her up, it seemed, because she started for it and then moved past to my ankles. And after she'd finished them, she went back to the bathroom.

When she came in again she brought clean water and another cloth.

I felt her hands on my thighs, her trying to nudge them apart—that's how I realized I was holding them tight together and couldn't seem not to. "Come on, baby," she was saying. "I need you to let me." And when this was too obtuse for me to follow, she said, "Come on, sweetheart. Just let me open your legs a little."

I felt them coming apart—from the force of her hands or my own inclination, I couldn't tell. Her hands did feel solid. Solid and sure and making me believe her, though maybe not wholly because I was trying to sit up and watch what she was doing.

Her face made me lie back again. She looked as pained as I felt. I fell back and tried not to cower, but this wasn't possible, it hurt too much. Seemed to hurt more than them having done it. And I was crying and struggling that same way—inside myself, but showing no outward sign of it.

And when I came up from this, came up for air, I moved in a jerky, jarred way that made her grab hold of my wrist. I drew back from the sting of her hand. She realized she'd hurt me because she let me loose right away and I pulled the rest of me back from her. I curled up afraid. Wanted the covers over me, but it would mean letting go of my knees. I'd hugged them tight to my chest and wouldn't let go.

She was trying to get me loose from myself. Did this first with words I could only hear bits of. I could only hear her saying, "Sweetheart," again and again until I couldn't even hear that.

I felt her though. I felt her hand stroking mine, stroking the back of it, the length of my fingers. And bit by bit I let her take it in hers. And once I'd let her do that, I let go of the rest of me.

She kissed my palm and then my wrist, stayed doing this before she moved to my stomach and then my thighs, and then between them. My body wanted her, while the rest of me didn't. My body maybe even needed her, needed what she was doing. And so this was another time it let me down.

I hadn't come off in that whole time with Burt and the others and so I told myself I had to have what she was giving me. Tried to tell myself the whole of me had to have it.

But I couldn't accomplish this. Even I couldn't make this all right, make her doing this right, her doing it now. And I couldn't stay away from what she might want or need. From what she might always have wanted and needed from me, when faced with me, with my need. From thinking that maybe this was the only way she'd known, ever, to help me.

She had to work at it but she did finally bring me off, though it happened in a dead, overdue way, not satisfying either of us.

Afterward, she seemed not to know what to do with herself, not right away, and this made me turn from her. I pulled the covers around me and drew into myself again.

I could hear her putting things away. Maybe I wanted for her to go away, but I couldn't be sure of this, and I sure couldn't have asked her to.

I do know that when she'd taken off her clothes and curled up behind me, I didn't want her anywhere near me. I pulled further inside myself. Tried to get far enough in there that I couldn't feel her arms and legs wrapped around me.

I couldn't do this or she wouldn't let me. And sleep wouldn't come either. I stayed rigid in her arms with her still trying to smooth me out. And I felt wrong about this, like I was betraying her. And while I knew I had this backward, it still didn't feel backward—even the thought of this, clear just a moment ago, turned unformed and gauzy, went slipping away.

I never did drift off. I didn't even pretend it very well. And I felt her struggling, too. Unable to settle herself or her body until finally she got up and I heard her dressing. And even though it was clear she knew I was awake, she said nothing to me before she left.

Now, with her gone, all my tautness turned to heaviness. And with sleep dragging me this hard I felt afraid, not simply unwilling. I felt a tiredness so big, I feared I'd never wake up from it. I couldn't fend it off, though. And when I went to it this time, I understood my fear. This time that black sleep was so endlessly empty it'd become the only place for me. The only place a person like me might want to stay.

Thirty

I did wake up. Woke up sore and feeling drugged and wishing I really was, but having no inclination to even find my liquor. I wanted to go back to that blackness where nothing ever happened or ever had. Wanted this the way a child wants death, or the way I had as a child. A want simply to stop it.

All this swimmed in my head and sent me swimming. Maybe that was the real trouble about what had happened last night. Maybe it'd brought me too close to something I'd always longed for. Opened me again to the idea of stopping it all instead of trying to outrun it. Or run around it. And always instead running into it again, running smack hard up against it. And each time, it hurting differently and more, leaving me running out of ways and things to deaden it, dull the blow.

Beth didn't call, not that day and not the next and not the whole week. And so I went into the next one wondering if she walked around in the same blurred dream as me, though really I wasn't doing much walking at all.

I wondered if she was. Then decided she was going through the motions of her life in a stunned sleep. I used this as a way to explain her not calling. Tried even to use this to keep her close to me, keep us someway together.

It didn't work very well, or very long. Really, it didn't work much at all. I kept at it, though. Kept it up another day or so even once I knew all the gaps and holes by heart.

What I did the day after that, in the early evening, was go to her. I couldn't not and couldn't think much about why, about what I intended. Not even once I got there.

I found her waiting on me as if the days, weeks really, hadn't occurred. And it was curious to me, the idea of her waiting this way every evening. It put me off balance, but when I regained my footing I found myself angry, and then knew I had been all along.

She met me at the door to her office, not the outside one. And right away I went at her. Physically, until we were clear across the room and I had her against the wall—crunched there between the wall and her desk.

I pulled and pushed at her. Got her half sitting on the desk, and then got my hand into her. I fucked her and fucked with her. I kept this up a long time. All of me pressed against her and into her, my mouth so near hers, but not kissing her.

I could hear her cries, which weren't the kind from pain. Her taking pleasure in this felt like failure and so I had to see I'd come here to hurt her in the way I'd always known hurt.

I finished her and then she slid down the wall, wound up slumped against it. I left her this way. Stumbled out her doors, craving that blackness, craving it physically.

A tingling tiredness pulled me forward, little clusters of needles in my thighs, behind my knees, pricking the soles of my feet. And there was this other tingling taking over my chest and growing beyond it. Hatred for loving her and for letting her love me. It pounded there, mingling with the want for blackness until I had to see these two things together—as part of each other.

With each step these blurred more, and when I got myself home and into my bed I couldn't sleep right away for knowing the relation. For seeing that I'd needed her help in the most conventional of ways. That all the rest had been about covering this. A way to try to put her where I put everyone else.

If I'd been able to do this, I wouldn't have had to see the very thing I wanted someone to take away. This specific hunger for nothingness. And when she'd shown me it instead? I'd wanted her to take it away, or replace it. Wanted her to be what made it all stop, but in a different way—one that'd let me be still, and still stay here.

And that she couldn't? That she hadn't been able and that nobody would've? And that she'd gone about it all wrong? That all of it between us had been terribly wrong from the first? None of this changed that she was first. I'd never be able to take that from her. Whether I spent the rest of my life loving or hating her, she'd always have me that way. Be the one who'd first had me. The closest I'd come.

Thirty-One

And maybe Beth had helped me because in the following days I found something killed my taste for it all. Not for that particular slumber, but for the little ways I'd tried to find it without admitting to it. I'd no pull to parking lots or bars, no interest it seemed.

I began living in a quiet way. I did this suddenly. But at the same time, I'd slipped so silently into it, I might never have noticed. Except, lately, this type of thing was all I did notice.

I'd like to say I used Ingrid's money, which was still there, and moved far away. I'd like to say I started over in this very concrete way, but that's not what happened.

I never did see Ingrid again. But I couldn't stop seeing Beth. I couldn't face losing her. Not when it seemed I was losing everything else.

We didn't have sex anymore, though. We didn't decide this or talk about it, we just simply stopped. And we didn't talk about having done this, or anything else that'd come before, or between us.

Things with her became conventional. Not in the way I'd wanted, but banal. She began to help me in rudimentary ways. Helped me get another job.

My life began to take this ordinary shape. But I had to work hard to keep it that way. To keep myself from seeping over these outlines, bleeding through them.

I made some friends at work. The kind you go have a drink with, which we did one night some months later at another bar, not that one I'd formerly frequented.

We were sitting on stools, laughing and talking engrossed in this way when Jeremy came in. I stood up when he stopped next to me, when he ordered his drink first, and then said hello to me.

I said something I don't remember, some kind of greeting and he put his hand on my ass in the most casual of ways, was telling me I looked good.

This probably all appeared pretty normal, and I could almost believe it was, except for the feeling I had, which was the same turned-on terror they'd left me with. That and the little vial he wore round his neck. It had a tight silver chain through the cap and this piece of me suspended there in sickly green fluid.

He took his drink and moved on. And the way he did this left me near to believing I wouldn't have gone with him if he'd asked me to. But I was too aware of his not having asked. And aware, too, that I had my hand in my pocket, fingering that bullet, which I carried everywhere with me now.

And so when one of the girls from the office nudged me and said, "Who's that?" in the way that means he's so good looking, I was slow to respond and they all took this as me mooning over him.

I stood there while they teased me. I played along and then waited out the rest of the evening because I didn't want to leave the place alone.

We all said good night out in the parking lot, and I found myself still distracted—looking for familiar cars, checking inside mine before I got in. I did this despite knowing that Jeremy was finished with me—that all of them were.

I went home knowing I wasn't finished with them, had only been pretending to be. And I went into my apartment, which was the same one, knowing I wasn't finished with Beth either, with that ancient thing she'd let loose in me. That it wasn't gone but was lying dormant. I had the urge to call her and with this deadness inside knowing not to.

I carried that deadness to bed with me. And I carried with it a knowledge I'd had all along. That I should've died that night—it'd been the best chance I'd had so far. And that I hadn't? Hadn't taken it? It wasn't the relief or comfort I believed it ought to be. It was only a postponement of some kind. A cruel kind of cheat, pressing me to decide it myself.

I'd been left with two courses: do it myself, or undo the things that had put the desire in me to begin with. And it still smarted to see what I'd been up to for years. To see my life—pretty much all of it—as simply about finding someone who'd do me in, do me in for me. Especially it stung because I'd clung tight to an idea of myself as someone who wanted so much to stay alive. Saw myself cheating death, not it cheating me.

And so I lay in my bed, humbled and discouraged because I knew I wasn't up to offing myself, and I couldn't see a way to start toward the other passage.

I knew Beth had been an attempt. But right now this only reminded me I wasn't capable. She'd shown me what I had to face, but then made me see I was nowhere near ready to. That looking at a little bit of it pushed me back to needing to die. I'd seen it this time. I hadn't been able not to. And while this maybe should've felt like progress, maybe was progress, it seemed more like loss.

And so, with it too soon for doing things differently and too late to do them the same, all I could do was stay in this stasis, unable to live in the way I had for so long, to live a life all about looking for death while pretending survival. But not yet able to live any way else.

That familiar heaviness crept into my limbs as I thought these things. It began to take me over, and then turn me over, until I lay mostly on my stomach with the pillows pulled close and me huddled into them.

The blackness came behind the heaviness. Came on comforting and big as always. But not deathly. Not exactly. Not for tonight at least. And this let me believe I could maybe just dip into it. For little bits of time. Go to it without that eerie pull to stay and, in this way, maybe get some rest. Get some actual sleep that might start me mending.

So I went to it, greedy as always. But, even with that slumber taking me over, and then taking me under, I knew that leviathan thing slept in this same darkness. Lay with me, too. Resting, biding its time.

ABOUT THE AUTHORS

Heather Lewis was born in 1962 and attended Sarah Lawrence College. She was the author of *House Rules* and *The Second Suspect*, and contributed to several anthologies. She ended her life in 2002.

Melissa Febos is the author of four books, including the nationally bestselling essay collection *Girlhood*, which was a LAMBDA Literary Award finalist, winner of the National Book Critics Circle Award in Criticism, and named a notable book of 2021 by NPR, *Time*, the *Washington Post*, and others. Her craft book, *Body Work* (2022), was also a national bestseller, an *LA Times* bestseller, and an Indie Next Pick. Her fifth book, *The Dry Season*, is forthcoming.